Ways Home

Stories by
Karen Lee Boren

Flexible Press
Minneapolis, Minnesota, 2025

Print ISBN: 979-8-9914928-6-7
eBook ISBN: 979-8-9914928-7-4

Flexible Press LLC
Minneapolis, Minnesota
www.flexiblepub.com
Editors William E Burleson
Vicki Adang, Mark My Words Editorial Services, LLC

"No one does girls ready to brawl better than Karen Lee Boren. This world is one overlooked, an upper Midwest peopled by the half hopeful, half resentful, who steer, knowing they better be ready to fight or at least look ready. The language bangs out toughness and rock 'n' roll and not-a-lot-of life options and makes you nod—yeah, that's real."
—Margaret Dawe, author of *Nissequott*

"This is why we read short fiction! These stories throw you in the passenger seat beside real and realized characters who scream at you, cheat on you, plot your murder, and abandon you, but you will love them anyway. Boren's collection dazzles in range and scope, with stories that arc lifetimes to flash pieces that explode mere seconds. These pages are soaked through with wisdom, and every story asks dire questions and leaves you thinking, questioning, wondering. Intense, brutal, hopeful, and true, *Ways Home* keeps coming for you, and it will get you."
—Mark Polanzak, author of *The OK End of Funny Town*

"On the move, these stories walk, trot, race, searching for that ephemeral thing called home. Open and curious in parts, windswept and melancholic in others, characters in this collection come together to remind us that no place is ever enough for the vagrant human heart. Physical, rhythmic, touched by desire."
—Meher Manda, writer of *Jamun Ka Ped*

Table of Contents

These stories originally appeared, sometimes in different form, in the following publications: "By Any Other" in *Notre Dame Review*, "Dancing Around It" in *Obelus Journal*, "Breakneck" in *Flexible Persona*, "Crosshairs" in *Crack the Spine*, and "Veronique Offered a Toe" in *The Offbeat*.

Ways Home

Scenic
Routes

By Any Other

It is the autumn Joleen's name shoots to number one on the country charts, crosses over, and peaks at sixty on the pop charts. It will be weeks before Joleen finds out Dolly Parton spelled the name differently; by then it will be too late, but Joleen will nurse that small anomaly like a robin's egg found in the woods, blue and fragile. Now though, in the freak heat of a 90-degree October afternoon, at seven minutes after the hour, every sweltering hour, Dolly's voice cuts through the humidity and brands Jolene a man-stealer. From FM, AM, country, and pop stations, with a thumb-picked guitar riff and a lyric catchy as all get-out, Jolene cuts in.

Jiggs Hopson is the first to ride his bike past Joleen's house, scream-singing, "Jo-lene! Jo-lene, Jo-lene! Joooow-lee-ee-eene!"

Joleen dashes to the screen door to see him pedal up the hill to the corner, his pals, Horace Manfred and Dem Oster, straining at his heels. At the top, the three boys steer wide circles in the intersection. Then they let loose, Jiggs first, as always, Horace and Dem aping. They raise their hands from the handlebars to the cloudless sky. Joleen steps to the edge of the porch in time to watch them bullet down the hill, hair whipping, fingers fanning the wind. The luscious breeze of their descent cools her own flushed cheeks. As they pass her house, with barely a note change in their voices, all three scream-sing.

"Jo-lene! Jo-lene, Jo-lene! Joooow-lee-ee-eene!"

Joleen sucks the tip of her thumb, tasting the pink ladies she'd peeled for the apple butter her mom wants to serve with the evening's pork chops. Behind her thumb she smiles at the tartness and the attention. Jiggs is sort of a jerk, Horace shy, but last spring she liked Dem a lot. He has a cute smile now that his braces are off. They were on swim team together until he quit to hang out with Jiggs and Horace after school on Lake Milfoil's banks, sipping whiskey and smoking weed. Or so Tish Bennet says. Joleen still gives gossip some respect. *Smoke signals fire, don't it?* Tish has a habit of saying this whenever someone challenges her gossip, and for now Joleen supposes Tish is right.

The boys U-turn at the bottom of the hill and pedal up again, their breathing too heavy to sing, but they glance up and see her on the porch. Dem stands on his bike's pedals, pulling at the handlebars to help him up the hill, but he manages a two-finger wave as he passes her. Was it a wave? For years, Joleen will analyze that gesture and her own reaction, which is to keep teething her thumb, her fist hiding her smile and her wisp of delight. *They are thinking of me, seeing me.* She feels more like herself than ever before.

Later, each of the hundreds of times she replays this moment, she will insist that if she had uncurled herself, waved back, open and friendly, if she'd yelled "Hey, hey!" to Dem, maybe gotten him to stop and talk with her about swimming, asked the boys in for iced tea, if she hadn't furtively nursed her pleasure at their attention, things would have been different. Wouldn't they? The question always follows the certainty. *They would. Wouldn't they?*

At the top of the hill, the boys buck and rear their bikes like the colts in the fields, jolting into the air as if electrified. All at once, Horace and Dem shoot down the hill again, hoofing and bucking still, and howling her name. "Jooooooooo-leeeen!"

But Jiggs, a hard boy from a hard family, his face stained with freckles that do nothing to soften his manner, rides his bike's break, jittering halfway down the hill, slowing in front of her house, in front of *her*, to steer figure eights. His eyes spot her as he turns like a dancer spinning pirouettes. He grabs her gaze and holds, grabs and holds, chiseling infinity curves into her memory with his bike tires.

"Jo-lene, Jo-lene . . ."

His voice is more jump rope sing-song than howl, and she can't help noticing, with growing uneasiness, that he may actually be able to carry a tune, which he does, replacing Dolly's pleading lyrics with accusation.

". . . Jo-lene, you *slu-uh-uht*. You're the biggest *slut* in the whole damn world."

If I'd just lifted my hand. Just called out to Dem.

They might have seen her as the girl they'd known since first grade. She might have been a girl to them for a while longer, maybe until the song fell off the charts.

But *slut* hits her like a stone spit from his tires. She runs inside, the screen door slapping shut behind her. In the kitchen, she gulps apple-and-cinnamon-scented air. From the small radio on the shelf above the sink, Dolly's voice trembles piteously.

#

"Jolene" is number one through the holiday dances, New Year's Eve parties, and Valentine's Day. Nineteen weeks, all told.

To Joleen's misfortune, over the summer her best friend, Dora, moved to Charlotte, so Joleen started the school year odd girl out and hasn't yet settled into a new set of friends. Until Dolly's song hit, Joleen hadn't minded much. She's friendly with everyone at Privy High and considers herself well liked. She has a few swim team pals she hangs with at meets. Babysitting jobs keep her busy on the weekends. She likes to keep busy, and she likes school. She has a small talent for drawing, but she considers herself too boring to be an artist. Don't artists have to be flamboyant and daring? Like Dolly. When Joleen bothers to think ahead, she imagines herself in retail or in restaurants, maybe nursing in a hospital, someplace where she can exercise her friendly nature, be helpful.

But since Dolly's hit song, with no fixed set of friends to deflect, protect, and sympathize with her when a herd of boys sings at her as she walks down the school hallway—using not just Jiggs's lyrics but also replacing the word *slut* with *whore, bitch, slag, skeeve, beaver,* and finally, *cunt*—no one is there to back-talk the boys with or for her.

Retorts materialize only in the sleepless, wee-hour darkness of her bedroom. She writes the curt putdowns in her calculus notebook. *Jerk, idiot, douche bag.* Surprisingly, she pictures Dem, not Jiggs, when she mentally spits the words, which aren't nearly as bad as what the boys call her. *Prick, dick, fucker.* Still not as bad, but she couldn't bring herself to say them anyway.

Exhausted, she questions if clever or bitchy is the way to go. After all, she doesn't want an exchange of insults. She wants to right their vision so they see she's been misidentified; she's not that song girl. *It's not my name. It's not even spelled the same. I'm* een, *not* ene. *My eyes are brown, not emerald. My hair is the color of walnuts.*

Over breakfast that morning, seeing the bags under her daughter's eyes and her slumped disposition, her mother reminds Joleen that she's named after her French great-grandmother, Jolie.

"Your name means pretty in French, *jolie*," her mother says. "And you were the prettiest baby. You *are* the prettiest girl. Inside and out. You can't let a stupid song define you. You just ignore them, honey," her mother says. "Those boys. They just want attention." Her tone is kind but firm, suggesting things would have to be much worse for her to intervene.

Joleen knows her parents believe in letting kids solve their own problems. She doesn't really disagree. What could they do? They can't come to school with her and walk her from class to class. Can't threaten the boys who sing, or even request the school censor them.

"Stand up for yourself," her father says. He drops his spoon into his empty cereal bowl and swishes a fist through the air, trying to joke her out of her misery. "You want me to teach you how to box?"

Until Dolly's song, she believed that if she ever had to stand up for herself, she could. And she wants to stand up for herself.

"Oh, Dad," she says, smiling to please him.

She touches the notebook where she's written her retorts and refutations, but the paper is dry from the heat and cuts her skin.

That afternoon, she fails her calculus test. She stares at the red *F*, shocked that this grade represents her. She may not be brilliant, but she's no *F*. She's just been so distracted lately and slept so poorly. Mrs. Larsen had shaken her head as she handed the test paper to Joleen.

Joleen's so busy trying to reconcile this failure with the girl she's understood herself to be that she isn't ready for the boys who come singing. They screech like owls, whoop-whooping skyward, their bodies springing into the air, ricocheting off the metal lockers that line the hallway. Her muscles tense at their crashing sounds. Sweat soaks her skin, blood blotches her cheeks. She tries to summon her strength, but with her failure in her hand, her shame on their lips, all she can manage, the absolute best she can do, is bite hard and hold back tears of bafflement. She gapes at the boys, who barely look at her. They used to be nice boys. They used to be friendly to her. Her throat becomes a snail shell, a hard, twisted place into which her voice shrinks.

After this, girls who might have allowed Joleen into their circle before Dolly's song avoid her. She supposes they suppose that Tish Bennet's truism is true. *Smoke signals fire, don't it?* Actually, when Joleen breaks it down, she finds the nice girls avoid her, which is as much kindness as they can afford without smudging their own reputations. The rougher girls, the female equivalents of Jiggs, in spirit if not in family, adopt his lyrics. They whisper-sing as they pass her, their husky breaths wafting with scents of their body powders. After nineteen weeks, once the song is falling on the charts, they don't bother to sing. Her name is enough.

"*Jooooleeeene . . .*" they hiss.

One of Joleen's swim team pals, *former* swim team pals, Laurie Garland, says within earshot of Joleen, "She tries anything with my boyfriend? I'll cut her dead." She runs her finger over a lump in the pocket of her swimming duffel that suggests a switchblade, yet is more likely a lipstick. But still. The message is clear. Joleen is a slut. Joleen is not to be trusted. Joleen is a Jolene.

How has it happened, Joleen marvels, that she's woken up one day, and by no action of her own, she's become someone, some*thing* really, that everyone in the world can agree, that she herself agrees, is hateful?

I'm een, *not* ene, she insists silently. No one hears her. Eventually not even herself.

Joleen becomes the class whore, a seductress, and man-stealer before her first kiss.

Later, when the char has somewhat rubbed off, when Dolly's song has dribbled down the charts, girls still avoid her, especially those with boyfriends. Her babysitting jobs dry up. She'll never know for sure if what she suspects is true: Wives don't want to risk a Jolene around their husbands. She takes to wearing blousy shirts in busy patterns and maxi-skirts to hide her body. She walks with her shoulders slumped, curling her spine as if trying to crawl inside that twisted shell at her throat. She gets a job washing dishes weekend nights at a supper club, called Cruise Inn, in the next town over, where she's hidden in the darkest part of the kitchen; no one bothers to call her more than *Hey You There.*

During breaks, she gazes through the windows at the spotlit performers on stage who sing has-been songs, "I Only Have Eyes for You," "Chances Are," and "My Kind of Girl." The sweetness of them sickens her with longing. When her break is over, the spotlight blanching her vision, she can barely see the gnawed steak bones and smears of au gratin she scrapes into the trash. Alone in the car, driving home in the dark, she sings the songs, off-key and open-throated.

Before she graduates high school, only one boy asks Joleen out. She detects a leer in his gap-toothed smile, like the one she'd seen on Jiggs's face as he figure-eighted in her street, and says no.

No dates, no movies, no dances, no parties. Instead, she studies. She banks her dishwashing money. She is the first student in her class to submit her application to the state university 300 miles away.

During the rest of her high school time, despite everything, Dem is the boy she most longs for. *If I'd just lifted my hand.* Sometimes he glances at her in Latin class. She searches out an apology in his expression. Longing aside, she feels owed one, by him more than Jiggs. Jiggs, she believes, was simply being A Jiggs. But she recognizes Dem as malleable. He'd been her teammate, a near pal. She'd liked him. Okay, he hadn't been the first to spit dirt on her; Jiggs had done that, but Dem hadn't contradicted Jiggs. He'd waited at the bottom of the hill for Jiggs and ridden off with him, laughing and joyous. Free in his bike-loosened limbs. A colt galloping with the herd. He stayed Jiggs's friend for the best part of the year when the Jolene/een hating was at its peak.

Toward the end of that first school year, Horace's family had moved away. Jiggs had gotten arrested for selling pot soaked in brandy and baked dry. He'd been sent to the Marsh Valley Juvenile Detention Center, and although he was probably out by their junior year, he hadn't returned to Privy High.

By the time of Jiggs's arrest, Dem had already been distancing himself from Jiggs, having joined track and the math club. Now, in their senior year, Dem is popular, and teachers seem to like him. Jiggs's criminal behavior hasn't left a mark on Dem.

Joleen resents that Dem's been allowed to cover his bad acts like new snow over a manure pile, while she remains not just Joleen, but "A Jolene." Slut. Whore. It's a given that she's not to be trusted. Yes, she wants an apology for Dem's part in her misery. More than an apology though, she would like him to acknowledge that he understands the unfairness of this difference, that like Jolene, he got to make a choice. *"Whatever you decide to do . . ."* Like the song's speaker, Joleen didn't have any say in her own change, but Dem did.

One day in Latin class, Dem's bored gaze lingers on her. Her mind flashes to being on that porch again, this time imaging herself pulling her thumb from her mouth and waving. In her mind, he meets her wave with his smile, a skid of his breaks, and a laugh that dismisses the stupid Dolly Parton song. Hadn't he lifted those two fingers at her as he pumped up the hill?

Could that gesture of friendliness work now? Dem's popularity would go a long way to washing out Dolly's stain. If others see him see her differently, they may adjust their visions too. In a burst of courage, of *audacia*, she raises her palm toward him.

Startled, his gaze shoots back to the Latin translations on the board, *culpo/culpas/culpat*, as fast as his bike had bulleted down the hill in front of her house.

In the hallway after class, Dem French-kisses Sheila Fitzwold in plain view. As Joleen watches, trying to understand him, his eyes slide in her direction. Still kissing Sheila, he waggles two fingers at Joleen, the sign the boys use for fingering a girl. Joleen backs down the hallway, feeling guilty and confused and humiliated for once again running away when she has done nothing.

Joleen graduates high school unkissed, a straight-A student, a stack of dishwashing money in the bank.

That summer she spends hot afternoons when she isn't working at Cruise Inn swaying in her backyard on the bench swing. She doesn't dare sit on the front porch. She's abandoned the thought of a job in retail or nursing as she'd intended before Dolly's song. Instead, she plans to declare accounting, the least sexy profession she can imagine and probably easy for her now that she earns top marks in math. But her studies are not on her mind as she swings.

She dreams of friendships with people as different as possible from the kids with whom she went to high school. She hopes her new college friends will never have heard of Dolly's song, but she's not taking any chances. New place, new name.

She considers Josie, but fears association with the cartoon band. That's all she needs, to be branded a Pussycat, which would surely be minus the *cat* in no time. As she swings, she finds there are countless name traps. Her middle name, Alice, is out. The still-recent a novel about a 15-year-old druggie runaway is the obvious association, reinforced by another goddamned song, this one by Jefferson Airplane.

She empathizes with kids saddled with *Adolf* in the thirties, *Oswald* before 1964. Pity the baby girls named *Cleopatra, Delilah, Jezebel,* or *Sheeba*. Of course, any decent parents wouldn't name their children these names now, but there's no telling what can happen. Poor *Roxanne, Lucille, Sharona, Sally, Maggie May, Cecilia*. To name a few.

She considers using her grandmother's name, *Jolie*, but French has its own sexy associations. She can't risk it. *Julie's* out too; people singing Bobby Sherman's earworm of insecurity to her would drive her mad: "Julie, Julie, Julie, Do You Love Me?"

"I hope she does leave him," she says of the song's singer to the birch trees, who breezily nod their agreement.

She returns to that moment on the porch often, picking at her own guilt. That day on the porch, she'd taken such pleasure in being seen and named by the three boys. All she wants now is invisibility. She wonders how to go about becoming nameless, a pronoun perhaps, rather than an always-improper proper noun. But barring this, better to choose your own name, she supposes.

Joleen enters university calling herself *Leena*.

To her delight, her roommate, Annie, takes Joleen under her wing. Despite Annie having something of Jiggs's hardness, or maybe because of this hardness, Joleen admires Annie. Annie has a tattoo of a mermaid and a navel ring decades before these body alterations are mundane. She alternately wears pink and purple DayGlo outfits and ripped-up black clothes spattered with paint. She frizzes her hair and uses Kool-Aid and Final Net to create wild sculptures that leave her pillow burnished.

At first, Joleen's shocked, which delights Annie. Shocking Joleen becomes Annie's pastime, and she takes Joleen to clubs that shiver with music closer to the sound of chainsaws than to anything Dolly's ever sung. Under the guidance of her roommate, Joleen skates the periphery of the punk scene, such as it is 300 miles from Privy, watered down but earnest. She loves the names of the clubs Annie takes her to: Bottom Barrel, Stained Pits, Junk Yard. Her favorite is Dirty Downstairs, a tiny box of a place with glossy-black walls scarred with penis and boob graffiti, fists whipping the bird, cartoon characters mooning.

Bathed in the tuneless noise of live performances, the shell at Joleen's throat untwists. She slams her body against other bodies. In the tangle of limbs and torsos, her own tension lets go. Only now does she realize just how tightly she's held herself since that day when Jiggs and Dem rode down her street, screaming her name. She screams now, the shell at her throat shattering with the vibrations of every obscene slur once hissed or spit at her. The club's blackness swallows her anger and begs for more.

Over spring break, Annie visits a friend in D.C. and hears Patti Smith sing Dolly's song at the Cellar Door.

"It was, like, revolutionary. You should have been there, Leena!" Annie says. "Every song Patti sings is a feminist fucking anthem just because she's singing it."

Joleen says nothing. Annie's her first friend since Dora moved away. But Annie still doesn't know Joleen's real name. Of course, Joleen avoids the students here from Privy High, who hang together in a protective pack, which includes Sheila Fitzwold and Tish Bennett. One day, when Joleen dashes into the dining hall to grab coffee before her economics class, she imagines she sees Dem with Sheila. She ducks out a side door, the old shell at her throat twisting shut with relief and anger that even an imagined Dem has intruded. This is supposed to be *her* new start.

But reinventing herself is harder than she thought. Every official piece of mail comes emblazoned with her seductress name, so she collects her mail in the early mornings or late nights when everyone is sleeping or partying. But each class attendance sheet lists her as *Joleen*, and no matter how often she corrects them—"It's *Leena.*"—professors persist in calling her by the name on their roll sheet. One day in her principles of accounting class, the teaching assistant calls on her by singing her name. Two notes. Dolly's notes. He smiles at her innocently enough, but those two notes stun her into silence.

She immediately drops the class. All the classes in her major are full, so she signs up for an elective life-drawing class.

The students sit in a circle, sketch paper attached to easels. At first when the models, males and females on alternate class sessions, drop their robes and adopt various revealing poses, Joleen is too embarrassed to look at them. Their nakedness reveals her own, and her cheeks burn with shame as they had that day on the porch. Then her teacher appears at her side. The corpulent woman, with sheered hair the color of steel, guides Joleen's hand over the paper. Joleen smells patchouli without knowing what it is.

"Just lines and curves, shadow and light," the woman says, her fingers warm on Joleen's fist. "Close your eyes. Forget the bodies. Imagine the lines. Now, open your freshened eyes."

"Oh," Joleen says, her hand moving to capture the lines with her chalk. This separation of flesh and shape gives her a different kind of release from that day Jiggs pirouetted in front of her house, different than dancing at the clubs gives her. As her hand moves across the page, Jiggs appears in her mind. But this time, it isn't his words or the notes she remembers, but the infinity shape he carved with his bike tires, the light inside and outside the figure eight. She reduces him to a thing she can capture and pin onto the page; when she draws his face, she takes extra care with his ugliest features.

After class, she goes directly to the art department's office and changes her major. She rushes back to her dorm room, excited to tell Annie her news. She's going to be an artist. A theater major herself, Annie's sure to be excited about the change.

When she walks in though, Annie's singing Dolly's song.

"This came for you, and the RA brought it up because it's too big for the mailbox."

Annie gestures to a brown box, likely a care package from Joleen's mother. Unbelievably, her mother addressed it using Joleen's full name.

Annie continues singing.

"Stop singing that," Joleen says.

"What? Oh, I didn't know was doing it. It's catchy, you know?"

"Yeah, I know. Could you stop?"

"Did I tell you I heard Patti Smith sing it at the Cellar Door? It was a fucking fem—"

"You told me. A hundred times. Could you stop already?"

Annie shrugs and stops singing, but from here on she calls Joleen her by her full name. In no time, so does everyone on her dorm floor, and the song inevitably follows. Joleen tries correcting people for a time.

"It's *Leena.*"

But *Jolene* sticks.

"It's just a song," Annie says when Joleen complains. "I mean, it's not like it's about you, right?"

"Yeah, sure," Joleen says, but becomes petulant and moody around Annie and everyone else on her dorm floor. She's happy only when she's in her studio, drawing or painting or building sculptures that allow her to hammer things. Or at the clubs where her surliness is accepted without question. By the end of the school year, she and Annie are barely speaking.

Over the summer, Annie writes to Joleen about getting a new boyfriend. *I'm in love!* Then she stops writing, not even a postcard to let Joleen know she's requested a different roommate for the next school year.

Joleen moves off campus alone, into a small studio apartment, telling her parents it will be easier to study, telling herself the solitude will feed her art.

For the next few years, although Joleen knows it's bad for her, like the cigarettes she now smokes, like the whiskey-neat that becomes her signature drink, she follows Dolly's career, which skyrockets. Dolly's platinum-hair jungle, the boobs, the lips, red and plump as those pink lady apples Joleen peeled years ago, get whiter, higher, redder. Dolly writes and records so many hits that "Jolene" might well have become one of the many. Except other singers keep recording it. Pop singers, Persian singers, Scottish, Icelandic, Australian. Parodies, duets, a cappella versions appear. Stripped down, sped up, acoustic, electronic, raps. In genre after genre, in languages Joleen has barely heard of, Jolene's emerald eyes and auburn hair seduce another woman's man.

"Fuck," Joleen says years later when the song springs up in an animated television show. She snaps off the TV and turns the screen to the wall.

After Annie, Jolene again finds it hard to make friends. As a *Jolene*, Joleen can't be trusted, but neither can she trust easily. If all it took was guilt by association to turn her into someone she wasn't, how can she be sure someone else won't turn on her just as sharply? Hadn't Dem? Hadn't Annie?

Without Annie (who this year seems to have discarded punk for what looks to be disco freak, *so chic*; Joleen sees her crossing the quad, wearing purple sequined pants and strappy lamé stilettos), Joleen continues to frequent the dingy music clubs. She goes from never having been kissed to fucking over the bathroom sinks with guys who rarely bother to ask her name. She rarely asks theirs and never asks if they have girlfriends. Why should she, she asks herself as she reapplies bruise-colored lipstick in the bathroom mirror after an encounter with a pimply guy with crimson fingernail polish. I'm a *Jolene*.

She still likes Dirty Downstairs best, and while she can't say she has friends there exactly, she's gained the grudging acceptance of familiarity. On DD's wall, near her favorite bar seat, she's markered a bicycle, the wheels two glaring eyes. She especially likes the open-stage nights at DD when new singers, off their heads with booze or drugs, get up and scream out their pain in foul language, the harsher, the better. One night, the bartender, Nicko, gives her free shots, then talks her into going on stage. She yells out "Jigsaw Feeling," getting half the lyrics wrong, but feeling purged when she stumbles off stage.

One Saturday night though, instead of going to Dirty Downstairs, she buys a ticket to Dolly Parton's concert. She dresses with care in her most ripped-up black jeans and a sleeveless T-shirt on which she's painted the same glaring bicycle image from DD's walls. She wears spiked wristbands and engineer boots. She slicks her lips black.

She's a standout in the crowd of cowboy hats and Western shirts with snaps and pointed collars. She wants to tell them all what their Saint Dolly has done to her. Although she gets plenty of stares, no one hassles her as she'd both worried and hoped they might. She's ready for a fight; she massages the lipstick bulge in her pocket menacingly. She sits silently in her seat surrounded by upright fans, swaying and clapping to "Dumb Blonde" and "Love Is Like a Butterfly."

Dolly saves her big hits for her encore, so Joleen buys beer after beer, waiting, seething. By the time the first notes of her name-song twang from Dolly's cave of a throat, Joleen's wasted, and she has to pee. She gets to her feet. On stage, Dolly's hair bounces. Her apple lips hang in the spotlight.

"You ruined my life," slurs Joleen. "You ruined my fucking life!"

The Dolly fans around her wrongly sympathize for her jilted past.

"Fuckin' Jolenes!"

They pump their fists in solidarity. The woman standing next to her pats her back.

"Home-wreckers. They're the worst."

"No," insists Joleen. The woman's high pigtails brush Joleen's cheek. "I'm her. I'm *her*."

"Yeah, me too! I hate bitches who steal. No pain like losing your man to another woman. You go ahead and sing it, girl."

Joleen stomps out of the concert, the slaps of her combat boots silenced by Dolly's belting "I Will Always Love You" at her back.

In the last month of her senior year, Joleen arrives late to DD's open-mic night, late even for DD. Her senior art show is coming up, and she's been absorbed in a found-materials sculpture. Every piece in her show is untitled.

Tonight, DD is satisfyingly crowded and hot. The heat of the other bodies mingles with her own sweat. When Nicko sees her, he ignores several customers and serves her whiskey without her having to ask.

She will miss DD when she graduates, but she's ready for a change of scene. With the help of the art professor who taught her first life-drawing class, she's already got plans to move to New York in a few weeks for a grunt job at a gallery, which is a damn sight better than going home to Privy.

"You getting on stage tonight?" Nicko asks, sliding a plastic cup into her hand.

The whiskey burns her throat with such satisfaction that she shrugs and says, "I'm tempted."

"I can't believe you're leaving," he says, ignoring the harangues of the other customers. "I'll miss you."

"Like an old shoe," she says, the phrase one her mother uses.

"I'm used to seeing you here."

Narrowing her eyes, she calculates the possibility of this truth.

"You going to come visit me in New York?" she says. More than DD, she realizes, it's Nicko she's going to miss.

"Tempted," he says as he moves on to serve a woman with five rings in her lip.

Joleen barely notices the singers who step on stage. Instead, she lets the vibrations of the guitars and drums bounce off and over her. As usual, open-stage night is a mix of done-up punks and a few normals who've come to gawk. She admires a woman's green mohawk spikes. Her own hair—now dyed blue—is too curly to spike, no matter how much hair spray she uses. The skeleton face paint on a guy so skinny his own bones tent his T-shirt is naff. The real fun though is the discomfort of the normals. Pretty people have no currency here, like the guy wearing a light blue polo shirt and a military-clean haircut, who'd be considered handsome in most settings. Here, he's nothing. He switches his beer from hand to hand, plugs his ear with his free fingers, and rumples his face against the sound.

"Shit," she says. "Dem."

At first she doesn't believe it's him until she visually scrapes the makeup off the naff skeleton and realizes it's Jiggs.

"What the hell?" she says as a song ends. Into the well of silence, she spits, "Fuck!"

"You okay?" Nicko pours her another drink as a new singer screeches.

Her first thought is to run as she had that day on the porch, as she had in the school hallways. She could escape out the back door. Nicko would help her.

The boy on stage, who looks no older than Dem and Jiggs had when they first rode past her house, squawks,

"Man-dick, pig-shit!" Jiggs thrashes; Dem shuffles, furtive and uncertain. When Dem looks her way, she gasps, her throat already clamping shut, but he scans past her without acknowledging her, returning his attention to the stage.

Anger rears in her. He didn't even see her. Her anger flares.

She remembers how material she felt that day when they first appeared on her street, singing her name. She'd felt so real, so seen. Why had she thought them seeing her made her real? Why had she thought they'd seen her at all? She'd been the one on the porch. They'd been performing, bucking and howling, fully in their bodies because she'd been looking at them. Later, Dem had done the kissing and the obscene gesturing while she gaped. *Her* seeing made *them* real, not the other way around. She'd breathed life into them, the way they're breathing life into that piss-ant singer on stage right now. The way the audience does to Dolly.

"Who are they?" asks Nicko, breaking into her thoughts. His hands are a flurry of flipping beer caps and shooting booze.

"No one," she says, a guitar scratch drowning her out. *It was never about me, it had nothing to do with me.*

Nicko cups his ear.

"No one!" she shouts.

"Just say the word, and they're gone."

He means it, she can tell. Nicko's known her for years now, seen her drunk and emerging from the bathroom after going with some guy. He saw her crap performance on stage. He's seen her passed out on the bar. And still.

"Look," she says, leaning over the bar and grasping his fingers, which still at her touch. "You have to come see me in New York, okay? You'll come see me?"

He grins. "I know a great place, Leena. Best music."

She's never heard him say her name before. She smiles back. "Can't wait. Right now, though, I gotta do something."

She hikes herself off her stool and skirts her way through the bodies, knocking shoulders, elbowing backs, shoving her way through the swarm of bodies until she reaches them. Up close, Jiggs is wirier than she remembered; Dem is thicker. She stands behind Dem, sees hairs sprouting up from his back and over his collar. She tries to think of a word, a name, that would make him feel all she has felt since that day on the porch. But there is nothing to say. She places her hand in the center of his back. His sweat-soaked polo shirt feels clammy against her fingertips, the flesh beneath spongy.

"*Nothing,*" she spits, shoving him.

He jerks forward but doesn't look at her.

Annoyed, she wipes her damp palm on her jeans and moves to the stage steps.

"I'm next," she orders Al, who's manning the signup sheet.

He shrugs and nods. She takes the stage while the other singer's notes still ring in their ears. She whispers the name of the song to the guitarist, who raises his eyebrows but assures her he knows it. The spotlight blinds her, but she blocks the light with her hand and spots Dem in the crowd. *Lines and curves, shadow and light.* She taps the mic, which squeals feedback. The crowd joyfully jeers, and she taps it again, shooting pain through every ear.

She opens her throat and growls, "This one's for the f-ing cheaters!"

Her voice gravel, she snarls, not Dolly's pathetic supplication, but her own iron-hot rage. The audience thrashes to the drumbeat, which is her heartbeat, steady and violent and seething. She grabs the microphone and Dem's gaze, waggling two fingers at him as he'd done in the hallway at school. Recognition widens his eyes. She tears open her shirt. The audience roars. She steps to the edge of the stage, Dem's gaze hooked. Her voice ripping, her body a steel-edged knife, she leaps, a stone spit from the porch, a blue robin's egg crashing to earth, her body heavy and hard and real.

Dancing Around It

I am sitting on the hood of my '79 Camaro trying to be fat. Not trying to get fat, which seems to be the case with Sherri, who is propped against my fender, and Lois, who leans over the hood. Both are eating greasy Kopp's cheeseburgers. I am trying to *be* fat. And Polish, really Polish. In short, I am trying to do my homework for Creative Movement 307 by imagining what it would be like to be my grandmother. Wouldn't you know it, just when I break down and take a class because it's famous for being easy, they shuffle the dance instructors like bingo balls, and I end up with one who insists we need to be "in touch with our inner history." Just play the goddamn music and give me my steps, is my attitude. I'll *grand jeté* better than any of those prissy ballerina-types. You know, the ones with pale skin and bony bodies who have been "living pretty" since they were five. I bet none of them have ever had a beer in their whole lives.

Anyway, that's what I'm doing right now, listening to Springsteen and drinking a Miller in the sun. It's one of those freak Milwaukee spring days when the weather is so warm it fools you into thinking summer's here. But Lake Michigan is as pale as the robe of the Virgin Mary herself, which means the water is still so cold that if you fell in, hypothermia would begin in seconds. Despite the fact that the lake wind is damn chilly, Lois and Sherri have put on their suede halter tops and are trying to get tan. Their fleshy shoulders look as if they've been slapped with cheap rouge.

"This is so great," says Sherri, looking in my side-view mirror and drawing on one more layer of black eyeliner. She's a bottle blonde, and as she leans over, I can see she's in pretty bad need of a root job. "Man, this summer is going to be one big party."

"You say that about every summer," I say. "And it's always the same—the beach and beer."

"I mean it this time. Did I tell you I'm moving in with Walker?"

"No way," says Lois, licking ketchup from the underside of her new fake fingernails. "Your Dad'll kill you."

"Fuck 'im. It's time I got some freedom, y'know?"

Sherri's been aching for freedom since she was fourteen, which is when we first started hanging out. Eight years later and I still don't know why she's so strangled, exactly. Nothing's ever been so bad at home. She's just one of those people who thinks the world is conspiring to confine them. School's a drag. Work's a drag. Everything but hanging out or driving is a drag.

I'm a little disappointed to hear she's hooking up with Walker. He's okay. At least no worse than any other guy any of us has chosen, but she's talked about escaping "this shitty city" from the day I met her in detention. She'd been caught smoking in the grotto by Sister Lourdette, and that same busy nun had busted me for violating the uniform dress code. Sherri and I sat in the back of the detention room by the windows, and as soon as Sister Roberts started grading algebra tests, Sherri passed me a piece of paper on which she had drawn an intricate sketch of Christ with his arms outstretched. She had written beneath it in neat script, "Christ the Redeemer, Rio de Janeiro, Brazil. TRAMPS LIKE US . . ."

I didn't know anything about Brazil, but I'd just fallen in love with Springsteen, so I wrote back "BABY WE WERE BORN TO RUN!!!" although I wasn't even sure if you could drive from Wisconsin to Brazil.

From then on, she always invited me to go with her on whatever bizarre adventure she was planning: Loch Ness, the Great Barrier Reef, Man Mo Temple. I was always non-committal, but that never seemed to bother her. I expected her to ditch this place hours after graduation, but she's still here, and it's getting harder to believe her when she talks about moving on.

Again thinking about my grandmother, I consider asking Sherri what it's like to be as heavy as she is. Her flesh is massive. It hangs like water balloons off her skeleton, even off her back bones. But it's never been clear if she thinks of herself as fat, only that she thinks of me as skinny, and I'm certainly not going to be the one to point out her bulk to her.

"I got a great job lined up," says Lois. "Data entry for Wisconsin Bell."

"Sounds awful." I try to picture myself sitting at a tiny desk entering numbers into a computer all day, dead from the wrists up. All that stillness would kill me.

"It pays big. No lie. Ten bucks an hour. That's more than minimum. And, y'know, the woman who interviewed me said if I stay there long enough, I could work up to supervisor or whatever," she says. "Man, I could be set. They got great beni's."

"Beni's?" Sherri says.

"Y'know, benefits. Health insurance and shit."

"Still sounds boring to me," I say.

"No more boring than all the dance classes you take . . . y'know, you're never going to get a job."

This is an old argument, and I decide not to pursue it again. Somehow it always ends up that my life and plans look much paler next to theirs, and I get depressed and surly for a week. Sometimes I want to insist that they at least try to dance, to feel what an absolute high moving your body can be. But they'd never do it, not even in a disco or at a wedding or someplace like that. So instead, I drink my beer and think about Busia. I never knew my grandfather, who died when the eighteen-wheeler he was driving was run off the road by a drunk driver. She died when I was ten, but I have vague memories of a robin's egg blue dress, big as a tent and weathered from years of washing. It's maybe the softest fabric I've ever touched. I play with the hem as she stands at the stove making ox tail soup, but I can't see any way to transfer this memory into a dance.

"C'mon, let's play Frisbee," Sherri says, and I leave Busia at the stove.

I was too drunk on beer and rays to do anything but watch television when I got back to my flat, and it turns out I couldn't even do that because I fell asleep. Now I'm in a bind because I've got to have something to present to my dance class tomorrow, and I'm drawing a total blank.

I scramble some eggs, make a salad, and sit on the couch with a legal pad and a felt tip pen. I figure if I make a list of all of the memories I have of Busia, I can choose one and create some kind of pantomime:

slow and arthritic

heavy

white anklets on slippered feet

faded rose-colored babushka

Looking over my list, I realize this is not the stuff of dances. Once again, I mentally return to her kitchen—the only place I can actually see her. Grubby wooden chairs with high backs surround a table. The plastic tablecloth covered with pink and white checks slides under my forearms as I drink milk from an old mayonnaise jar and watch Busia gnaw an ox tail bone. I remember the arthritis clearly. Her knuckles are gnarled, her fingers as swollen as the kielbasa links she served for breakfast, both smeared with grease. Watching her tongue dart around the blackened crevices of the ox tail joint, her sallow teeth gouging the meat, I am afraid she won't know when to stop, that she'll devour the flesh of her own distended fingers without even knowing it. I stare at the circle of milk at the bottom of my glass.

This is not helping. Certainly, this is not what grandmothers are supposed be like. Shouldn't they be sweet, with twinkling eyes and homemade sugar cookies? How can I possibly expose Busia to those proper ballerinas whose very leotards seem to be dripping money and culture? I decide I have no choice but to fake it.

\#

The next day I sit on the hardwood floor of the studio viewing grandmother after grandmother, and I don't feel so bad. All of these small breasts and skinny limbs pretending to nurture—hugging air, rocking empty arms—look ridiculous, especially when the images are tripled by the mirrors that cover three walls. When it's my turn, I fly around the studio, arms sweeping the air. I advance and retreat, pirouette slowly, and end with an explosion of *tour jetés*.

"She was a gypsy," I say to the questioning eyes. "She was very free." I figure this is vague enough to get me off the hook. I mean, it's not like Miss Shay could check or anything.

Theresa Kowiak dances next. She has black hair, which she claims has never been cut, flat cheeks, and a thick nose. Large boned, she is always the first female forced to switch roles when we are short a male dancer for a performance despite her long hair.

She gets up from the floor, folds her body into an imaginary chair, and stares over our heads. We wait for her to start rocking or cuddling as everyone else did, but she doesn't move. After about two minutes, I hear my classmates begin to shift uncomfortably. A few minutes more and it's unbearable. At least my dance wasn't this bad— she's just sitting there. I check to see if her thighs are trembling from the strain of supporting her upper body, but her muscles are rock solid, her shoulders stiff and hunched. Then I notice her eyes moving slightly, widening and narrowing, animating her face one moment, deadening it the next. Occasionally she lifts her right index finger and drops it onto the arm of the imaginary chair. Twice she purses her lips.

Five minutes later when she stands, her dance apparently completed, the image she had created with her body remains etched in the air. Her actual body slips lightly back to her seat on the floor. Its sudden buoyancy is shocking, but also a relief, like drinking water after ice cream.

I glance at Miss Shay and find her staring at the space where Theresa was and nodding her head. It's crazy, but she looks as though she might cry. When class is over, she makes six dancers stay, but Theresa is not one of us.

"I think you ladies need to work a little harder on today's assignment," she says. I watch her hands as she talks, envious of the lithe fingers and manicured nails. Her translucent skin is tight, and I wonder if her face falls when she takes her hair out of that bun.

"You've got the weekend to really find out about your grandmothers. I'm certain they were all remarkable people. Really try to discover them."

The six of us refuse to meet each other's eyes on the way to the locker room. Disapproval, while constant, is tough on most dancers, and it's understood that until we achieve approval, we will not discuss our dances. Without showering, I pull on my suede boots and a sweater and escape to my car.

Once I'm maneuvering the smooth stretch of Lincoln Memorial Drive, I put Busia out of my mind. Hell, it's the weekend. The weather is still deceptively warm, and Sherri and Lois said they'd be at the beach again. Although I cruise through North Point a few times, I don't see them. So I glide into a parking space near our usual hangout spot, crank the tunes, and climb the boulders that have been dumped along the shoreline for erosion control.

The lake is a deeper blue today, and white caps frost its surface, then explode over the breakwaters. The air is intoxicating, so thick it feels like it's stroking my tongue when I open my mouth. And the sun on my cheeks and forehead is sweet. As I listen to the slap of the waves against the boulders below me, I feel my flesh coming to life as though the whole winter has been an out-of-body experience or a long separation from a lover. I imagine the water in August when it's warmed up just enough for the brave to swim in. Three seasons of the year, its appearance is tempting, but even at its most temperate, it leaves your skin raw with cold, and the gentle pull of the current can fool you into swimming farther from shore than you should. A cramped calf has done in more than one strong swimmer.

I consider what Busia must have thought of the lake the first time she saw it. My father told me her family emigrated from Warsaw when she was sixteen or seventeen. She was Marfa Wazniewski then, but she died Martha. I don't know when the change took place. Never having seen pictures of her when she was young, I create my own image of sandy brown hair, narrow shoulders, and long, bowed legs. I see her standing on the cliffs that overlook the lake's bank on the south side of the city where I grew up. What a sight that must have been for her. Endless water and sky. She lived only blocks away from the lake for the rest of her life, so it must have become a part of her. Surely its pull was as strong for her as it is for me.

I bet the lake made her want to dance too, although the only time I remember her dancing, or even moving farther than from the stove to the kitchen table or shuffling her great bulk the three blocks to Holy Family Church, was at a polkafest. Max and the Merrymakers had finished the "Just Because Polka" and started a waltz when Busia shoved the tail end of a pierogi into her mouth and effortlessly scooped my four-year-old body into her arms. She must have been nearly seventy then, but she sashayed around the dance floor as easy as a memory. I had a dance instructor once who said the body never forgets. Even if it can no longer *do* what it used to do, the memory remains trapped, and Busia's memory was flawless.

I hear Sherri's motor bellowing before she enters the parking lot. Her muffler rusted off months ago, and she hasn't replaced it because she thinks the engine sounds tough.

"Hey," I say as she lumbers up the boulders with a six-pack of Lite beer in one hand. She is chunky but has a certain grace, as though she knows where each ounce of fat is at every moment. "Man, you're lucky the cops haven't ticketed you for noise pollution yet."

"I did get stopped one night, but the cop let me off after I sweet-talked him." She strikes a sexy pose and bats her heavily mascaraed eyelashes.

"Wonder what Walker'd say about that?"

"That son of a bitch? Shit, we broke up last night."

"I thought you were moving in?"

"So did I. Turns out he was doing the nasty with Angie Riccio. Can you believe it—Angie Riccio?"

She hands me a beer, and we toast her new freedom.

That night Sherri and I meet Lois at Harley's, one of the local biker taverns decked out with parts of old Harley-Davidson motorcycles. The barstools are scuffed leather cycle seats, a few with cissy bars. A First World War vintage bike is suspended from the ceiling over the bar's liquor rack. When the music is loud, the bike sways. Once after drinking all night, I dreamt that the ropes supporting it snapped while I was sitting at the bar and I was trapped underneath when it fell. I screamed and screamed, but I couldn't struggle out before I woke up.

Harley's is crowded tonight—studded leather jackets and tattoos everywhere—but we find an empty table to sit at in the back near the row of pool tables. Stained-glass Pabst Blue Ribbon lamps throw yellow circles of light onto the green felt and reflect from the colored balls. Men and a few women lean on cue sticks or circle the tables, solemnly eyeing shots. At the last table, a guy with a dragon tattoo on one bicep and chunky turquoise rings on each finger either adds to or doles from a huge wad of cash, depending on whether he wins or loses his bet on each shot.

"I hope Walker is here so I can ignore him," Sherri says. She pours each of us a glass of beer from a plastic pitcher.

"No beer. Vodka." I say, pronouncing it "vudka" as my father does. I have decided to be Busia all night, so I rearrange the huge scarf draped around my shoulders and try to decide what to make of these curious Americans.

"What the hell's with her?" Lois says.

"She's playing Polski woman," Sherri says.

"Huh?"

"Never mind," Sherri says. "There he is!"

Walker is near the bar, paging through the CDs in the jukebox, his face green in the neon light. He's wearing his usual black denim jeans and a T-shirt with a beer logo on it. I've always wondered if he gets those T-shirts free somewhere or if he actually goes into a store and buys something with "Bud Light" ironed across it. Sherri is straining not to look at him, but at the same time, she's trying to check if Angie's here.

"Hey," Sherri says to me, "take a cruise around and see if what's-her-face is with him."

"Listen, if you two go at it, I'm outa here," I say, slipping out of character.

"Yeah, yeah, you always say that, Borczynski."

"I mean it."

"Just go see." She pushes me so hard I nearly fall off my chair.

"All right," I say, once again Busia, "I go." I toss the end of my scarf around my neck and weave my way through the pool players, careful not to bump anyone in the middle of a shot. I don't see Angie, so I position myself at the bar to see where Walker will sit. While I wait, I order a shot of vodka and try to imagine seeing this place, these people, for the first time as Busia might. Would she think the serious beards and leather caps on many of the bikers look mangy or tough? Would she think the women in tight jeans and high heels are pretty or just cheap?

Of course, they wouldn't have looked like this in her day. They'd have been factory workers, immigrants like her. My dad's told me the Poles who moved here in the early days wanted to create a little Poland. Those who could afford to built their houses and businesses of foot-thick solid brick. They built to last, and many still stand today. But Busia's house was wood, a cheap "Polish flat" my dad called it, a structure ornamented with gables and pointed cusps that're all but disintegrating today. When I was little, I thought Busia was as much of a fixture in her tall wooden house as the glass chandeliers. Now I wonder if after her long migration, she felt she had arrived some-where, finally, or if she spent her life thinking of going somewhere else, or even back from where she'd come.

As I throw back the shot, an image flashes through my mind of Busia yelling at my father. It is summer, the atmos-phere in the kitchen is stifling, but the scarred linoleum is cool against my bare legs. My father looks as he always does when the reality of him is not there to contradict my memory—stomach flat, arms powerful, hair dark and thick. From the floor where I must be sitting or crawling, I see Busia hurl her fist through the air as though cutting an overgrown field with a machete. I watch the flesh of her upper arm flap against her breasts; my gaze follows a drop-let of sweat making a path from the black bush of her underarm hair to the yellowed elastic of her bra. I hear my father's exasperated voice, "Ma, listen, I *am* American. Christ!"

"What the hell are you doing?" Sherri slaps me lightly on the shoulder.

"Nothing."

"Well, did you see her?"

"No, I don't think she's here."

Lois points to the window that looks out on the parking lot. "Isn't that her piece-of-shit Trans Am pulling in?"

Sherri bends over the table where a couple is seated so she can look through the window. The woman at the table gets a clear shot of Sherri's left breast, but like most people faced with Sherri's bulk, the woman says nothing.

"It's her," Sherri says. "C'mon, we can get her before she even comes inside."

She and Lois rush toward the door, but I don't move. Sherri is halfway through before she realizes I'm not following. "C'mon," she says, motioning with her arm.

I shake my head and wave her on, but she pushes Lois aside and returns to me.

"What the hell?"

"I'm not getting into a fight for you," I say, picturing the guys in the bar gawking and yelling "cat fight" or "chick fight" the way they always do when women get physical. I picture the looks the other dancers would give me if I entered the studio on Monday with a black eye or propped my broken leg onto the barre. No thanks.

"It's only Angie Riccio," Sherri says. She has moved so close to me I can smell her hairspray. The whites of her eyes are shocking against her black eyeliner and caked eyelashes; her fleshy jowls tremble.

"Let it go," I say quietly.

I back away, but she moves even closer, eclipsing the rest of the bar. Droplets of sweat bead between her breasts. The heat of her body has overpowered the chemicals, and the musky scent now emanating from her is so familiar I could be smelling myself. Plump cheeks flushed, lips moist, nostrils slightly flared. I realize she is fiercely beautiful at this moment, full of power, like a racehorse ready to bust out of the gate.

"C'mon, it'll take ten minutes," she says. Her eyes are almost pleading, almost fearful, but I know she doesn't need me to take Angie. Or anyone else, for that matter.

"I'll wait for you in here," I say. I turn to the bar and order another shot.

"Chickenshit," she says. Her breath burns my cheek. She pushes through a group of denim vests and out the door. Lois follows.

I return to our table and watch pool. Between shots I glance at the door. Once I look out the window to make sure things haven't gotten out of hand, but I can't see anything beyond my own reflection in the glass. Watching more pool, I wish I played well enough to get into a game, but these guys don't play for fun. I finish the remainder of the beer, and still they have not returned, nor has Angie come in. After a few more games, I figure they must have ditched me, so I leave.

The parking lot is empty, no sign at all of Sherri or Lois or Angie. No sign at all of a fight. Just a few cars and a whole stable of bikes, most of them custom designed: Low Riders with intricate engraving, tricked-out motor and cycle parts, overlength forks—anything to set the rider apart.

I drive home slowly, praying I don't get stopped for drunk driving.

Every time the phone rings for the rest of the weekend, I think it will be Sherri calling to tell me what happened. Once it's my sister calling from Detroit. Another time it's my father asking me to dinner Monday night. Finally, I call Lois, who tells me that Angie saw Sherri waiting for her and just kept driving.

"Sherri's really pissed at you though," she says. "She thinks you think you're too good for us or something. Y'know, now that you're hanging out with those dancer-types and stuff."

"Just because I wouldn't get into a fight for her?"

"You know how she is. Anyway, you better call her."

I put off calling her all Sunday and instead spend a long time practicing *pliés* and *échappés*, using my couch as a barre. I concentrate solely on the contraction and extension of my muscles until the rhythm of *one*-two-three, *two*-two-three, *three*-two-three is all that exists.

After that I work on my Busia dance while I'm still limber. I pantomime cooking first, then try wrapping a babushka around my head and shuffling to church. I sneak peeks of myself in the full-length mirror in the hall, and I do look like an old lady, even a little bit like Busia. But I keep thinking how embarrassed I'd feel showing this to the other dancers. I may not know much about her, but I know Busia was more than a dirty old Polish woman like those who rove Little Poland hawking *oplatek* wafers in the bakeries at Christmastime. She had a whole life. But I can't even begin to imagine what she would have felt crossing through country after country, over a whole ocean and half of another country just to get here. Surely the feeling was one of lightness, freedom—*Baby, we were born to run!* I mean, she was leaving everything behind. But I tried free movement in my last dance, and it didn't get me anywhere.

Because it's getting late, I go for dignified. I forget about the Busia I know and think only about what movements will impress the other dancers. This is, after all, a creative movement class. So I choreograph what I think is an elegant piece with elaborate foot and arm work.

Monday afternoon we sit on the floor again watching more grandmothers. During each student's performance, I glance at Theresa Frankowiak to gauge her reaction, but her face is even less expressive than it was during her dance.

Most of the dances aren't much different from the last time, and I see Miss Shay shaking her head as each girl finishes. When it's my turn again, I perform my new dance, chanting words like *noble, regal,* and *stately* in my head as I move. Not even one flash of Busia passes through my mind. Still, I think it's going pretty well. A glance at Shay, though, and I see she is shaking her head as she did with the other dancers. I rush the final moves just to be done.

As I sit back down, Shay says, "Well, I guess it's time to move on." I can see we've disappointed her again.

In the dressing room after class, I make a point of changing next to Theresa. I watch her nail-bitten fingers strip away layers of black Lycra, trying to figure out what was okay about her dance and not about mine. Technically mine was a lot tougher. After all, how much skill does just sitting there take? She sees me watching her.

"What?" she says, resting a hand on her broad hip.

"Nothing," I say. "I just . . . I was just trying to figure out your grandmother dance."

"What's to figure out? My grandma had three strokes. After the last one she couldn't move."

"Oh, I'm sorry," I say, completely embarrassed now. I start undressing so I don't have to look at her.

"It's okay," she says. "It really was pretty weird after it happened."

"So she was . . . like, a vegetable, then?"

"No, she was there. Sometimes you just had to look really hard to find her because at first glance you'd miss her. Y'know, sometimes you'd think she was happy, but she was really sad or depressed or maybe even just hungry or something. It was easy to get it wrong, to project your own emotions on her."

"Oh," I say.

"Anyway, your dance was good too." She grabs her towel and heads for the shower, leaving me in the aisle, half-undressed.

I really mean to call Sherri after class, but I take too long getting ready, so I'm running late meeting my dad for dinner at Sasha's. It's a local restaurant we've been coming to my whole life, not fancy, but my father claims they have the only real czarnina in town. He's already there when I arrive and has ordered the duck-blood soup and beef pierogies for us both. When I first see him, leaning back in his chair and laughing with the young waitress, my memory has to take a moment to reconcile itself with reality. His essence is as familiar to me as the lake, but his particulars—bald head, immense stomach, rings of fat beneath his eyes, wrinkled hands—seem more and more foreign each time I see him. When he stands up and embraces me, the mixture of sweat and garlic and something unidentifiable rushes me back to childhood; he smells of Busia.

We eat slowly, tasting each morsel of food. After the meal, he leans back and sips boiled coffee with heavy cream, and I swear I can see Busia in the slack rings beneath his eyes.

"When did Busia change her name?" I say, adding Sweet'N Low to my own black coffee.

"Her name?"

"From Marfa to Martha," I say.

"I don't know that she ever changed it. Officially, I mean. It just sort of happened when she started making friends who weren't Polish." He stirs his coffee, churning the grounds. "You know she really wanted me to be an American boy, not Polish, so she tried to find friends for me who weren't Polish. Made a real effort to do that."

"Really?"

"I never liked any of them though. Who knows why. Maybe just because she wanted me to like them."

"Did she like it here . . . in Milwaukee, I mean?"

"I don't know that she ever said," he says. A small smile plays at his lips, and his eyes fix on the blank wall next to the table. It's clear he's conjuring some image of his mother, and I wonder which moment in time his mind has frozen her in. "Y'know," he continues, the smile still there, "she considered herself one of the lucky ones, even after your grampa died, even after the arthritis made every movement painful for her."

"Yeah? Why?"

"Probably for a lot of reasons, but I remember her saying once that she felt blessed because here was so much like there—the Old Country, she meant—but also because it was nothing like there either."

I don't have class the next morning, so I finally call Sherri. Her dad must be on third shift again at Ladish because he answers the phone.

"You don't know?" he says. "She left. Decided last weekend to drive down to Cleveland. She's got a couple cousins there. She left yesterday."

"Did she go alone?"

"Yeah. Her ma and I aren't too pleased about that, but it's about time she got her ass in gear to do something. I been on her all winter. Who knows, maybe she'll find a job or get herself married even, eh? Anyway, I'm surprised she didn't tell you she was going. But she'll probably call you when she gets settled."

I'm surprised too, shocked even. I feel a little guilty too because I was starting to think she'd never get it together to go anywhere. Her life seemed to be getting as heavy as her body, and I figured she'd end up working at the Pick 'n Save or at Ladish like her dad, something like that, something she never wanted to do. But now, even if she's only gone a week, and even if it's only to Cleveland, she still did it, she got somewhere. And already I can't wait to hear from her.

I've got so much energy now I can't sit still. So I put on my jogging shoes, shorts, and a sweatshirt. Most dancers don't run or ice skate or even swim because this can alter the strength and flexibility of the ankles and add stress to the knees. And a knee or ankle injury can end a dancer's career instantly. But I take my chances. I like to build up my endurance. It gives me an edge over the other dancers.

I run the path that follows the line of the cliffs above the lake. The air is wet and cold. Heavy white clouds press like a hand from above, making sure you believe in a god up there even when you can't find many traces of him down here. Inevitably, the wind has shifted, and it seems like winter again, the world drained of color. Choppy and gray, Lake Michigan doesn't roar like the ocean. It churns as if irritated. As I listen to my feet thumping steadily like the backbeat of a song, I wonder if Busia had regrets, but I realize I have no idea what she thought. I am no closer to her.

After a few miles, I come to a lookout and stop to stretch against the railing. I wish I had brought a quarter to put into the binoculars machine, although all you can see is water. My calves are tight, and I'm afraid of pulling a muscle, so I walk back toward home, veering off the path and onto the yellowed grass to peer over the edge of the cliff at the rocky slope below. A couple of kids, maybe six or seven years old, are on the shore, raking their fingers through the wet sand and pebbles. Like playful dogs, they run to show each other good finds, then separate and search on their own again.

I watch them for a moment, then look out at the expanse of water and sky. My own heavy breath is in sync with the sound of the breaking waves, and it seems natural to move to our rhythm. Because it feels right, I start to dance my Busia dance, slowly, relaxing the footwork and gestures. For once I don't think about the movements so much or what the other dancers or Shay might think, but the heavy air makes me think about Busia's cumbersome body. With that arthritis, every movement must have been a struggle against gravity.

I feel its pull as I roll through knees, hips, back and neck. I roll again and again until I am undulating like the waves. The movements are jerky, but my body feels smooth as though I am dancing in water. My toes press into the spongy grass, the soil's juice staining my white shoes. Bending forward at the waist, I billow my arms, loosening my fingers and wrists and elbows but straining between my shoulder blades. My limbs pump like wings, which I realize now are not as carefree or effortless as they appear to be but are tightly muscled and must work hard to keep the body in flight. Of course, birds' wings must work hard, I realize. They have to work against stillness, which is as much a part of movement as leaves or smoke or waves are a part of wind.

As I dance now, I don't think about Busia's movement but her stillness, her bulk, and I see Sherri's too, and it seems the more slowly I move, the more the image of Busia rises like seaweed suddenly loosened from the lake's floor. It's not until I reach the space between movement and stillness that she really surfaces, and I nearly feel her strangled muscles in the quivering and straining of my own, but I lose my balance, catching the toe of my shoe on the tip of a buried rock. As I fall, one knee jams into the rock's surface. The pain is sharp, and I try not to panic as I wait to see if it will swell. Eventually it becomes clear the rock has only scraped away a few layers of skin, and there will probably be a slight bruise. But my mind is racing with the possibilities of what might have happened, at the danger in those small movements.

As I cradle my knee in my arms, still hesitant to walk, I watch the two kids on the shore throwing their new-found treasures into the waves. The taller kid is able to skip her stones across the choppy surface, making them bound gracefully from wave to wave. The smaller girl's stones pop up and plop and sink only an arm's length from her sneakers, but she claps anyway and jumps up and down each time one makes it to the water. I clap too, delighted by what she can do, certain that propelling the stones forward, even just a little, is a lot.

Long Way Home

I.

In 1970, when she was thirty years old, Evelyn thought the world was ending. She decided this on the train to Chicago. She had spent the last five years in Kansas City, Missouri, having moved there with her husband, Al. She was now moving back to Chicago, alone, for good.

She would live in her mother's house, a solid structure in Wrigleyville, where she would make an effort to build a life. Her mother had taught her that one must always at least make an effort, and she would do so. But she had no enthusiasm. In fact, she barely bothered to think about her unasked for future life now that her real life had vanished.

Her real life. It was the life for which her youth had prepared her, the one which she had looked forward to, and which she had enjoyed, brief though it had been. *Vanished.* The word seemed appropriate when she thought of her husband's death and the loss of the baby she had not been sure she wanted until the miscarriage. *Vanished.* As though under the wave of a magician's wand. *Poof!*

Her husband, Al, had been killed in a car accident late one night. He was drunk, which was no surprise. He usually became drunk when they went out on the weekend, and so did she, although not recently. Beer and whiskey, whiskey and beer. It was what they always drank, what Al drank that night. After all, what was the harm? Al was not a mean inebriate like some men she knew. In fact, his solid form seemed to soften around the edges after he'd had a few. That evening he had been no more zealous in his drinking than on any other evening. The two of them had been listening to music at a jazz bar, music Evelyn liked but didn't love. She loved the polka music she could only hear back home in Chicago. But Kansas City was a jazz town; here she made do with jazz.

She and Al had met friends for dinner that night, Gloria and Edward Mantiko. After eating the large steaks so popular in Kansas City restaurants, the two couples decided to go to a new jazz club. Al was the one to suggest a club, but they all agreed. It was Friday night, and no one had to work the next day. Edward and Al worked at one of the forging factories on the edge of the city, while Evelyn worked in a typing pool at one of the downtown firms.

In the jazz bar, Evelyn enjoyed the music more than she expected she would. It was lively, the music and the place. People danced crazy dances she knew she could never manage. She could waltz or polka or Polish-hop. But this jerking and sliding of the body into all angles? The wild flexing and twisting? Never. Still, she enjoyed watching. She could get inside the music just by watching the dancers.

She liked one dancer in particular, a large woman with dark, almost black hair. Her skin was as pale as a baby's, which Evelyn thought was a clue that the woman dyed her hair. The woman's eyes were thick with false lashes and outlined in black lines which extended beyond the rims' outer edges, making her look like she belonged on an ancient Egyptian pyramid. The lids were frosted blue, and her fingernails were painted the same frosty blue. She wore a tight dress with large circles in no particular pattern. On her feet and halfway up her legs were shiny white boots with chunky heels.

Evelyn liked the look of the woman, but she liked the way she moved even more. The woman was not thin, not fat exactly, but certainly not thin. And she seemed to know where each bit of flesh was at all times and exactly how to get the greatest effect from each inch. When she shook, she let her breasts shinny nearly out of the top of her dress. Then she moved just enough in another direction so the wayward breasts were no longer even considered. Rather, her hips, swinging in a smooth figure eight, were the focus of anyone watching. The woman's movements were odd, Evelyn thought, yet elegant as well.

She watched the woman much of the night. She saw Al watching her at various times too, but she thought he didn't like the woman. Perhaps he didn't approve of her. He could sometimes be a prude. His mouth was drawn into the crooked line Evelyn saw on his face when he watched the Bears lose a football game or when he watched the student protesters on the evening news. She knew it as an expression of his disgust.

Because of this expression, she wasn't prepared to encounter him and the woman in the hallway to the restrooms. She certainly wasn't prepared to find him pressing his body close to that knowledgeable body, rubbing his hands over the circles of that tight dress. No, Evelyn wasn't prepared, or she might have done something then and there. She might have yelled at him or dug her heel into the bone of his instep or pulled the woman away from him by the hair as she had heard other women tell of doing. Instead, she went back to the table, having forgotten her full bladder.

Gloria and Edward, of whom she had just asked the whereabouts of the bathroom, gave her a strange look. But she sat down without explaining her absence, which had been far too brief for her to have used the facilities. She didn't know what to say. She waited for Al to return, pretending she couldn't hear Gloria or Edward over the music asking where Al was, then not asking any longer, having suspected.

In the hallway, Evelyn had been surprised but not shocked. This was the kind of thing Al often did. He liked women, he said. He said this to his friends, to her friends, to her. Over the years she had gotten used to his flirting. She had even come to accept he had affairs sometimes. What surprised her most was that after a while, she found she didn't mind all that much, especially after the first time she suspected. It never interfered with their own sex life, which was still active and satisfying, to her at least. And she didn't mind the time he spent away from her either. She liked being alone.

What she had found distasteful the first time was her own uncertainty. So after a month of picking up the telephone and hearing the receiver on the other end click down on her, she decided she must leave Al or make peace with this side of him. She had no faith that she could change him. Al was Al, after all, immutable as concrete.

Evelyn called her mother, who admitted Evelyn's father had plenty of affairs before he finally left them. She suspected Evelyn's grandfather had played around himself. "Although he had been a good husband in every other way, or at least a good father to me. Plenty of wives have put up with worse. But my girl, if you're going to leave, do it now *before* children."

Evenly decided to stay. After all, things might not be better with anyone else. Or with no one at all. Evelyn loved him, she supposed, despite his habit. Besides, now he was a known element, as her mother pointed out. She knew what to expect from him. Or she thought she did. This was really what had disturbed her in the hallway and continued to disturb her as the music tangled itself around her like an electrical cord: Al had done something unpredictable; she had misread his reaction to this woman completely. She wasn't at all his type!

Suddenly Evelyn couldn't stand the loud, chaotic music. The musicians had begun improvising, chasing each other with their notes, one note never catching up to another. Sly music, she thought with disgust, quirky and elusive. She found herself shaking her head as if to clear it, but the scudding and trilling sounds continued their assault.

"Polkas are so much better," she said softly. Tears pressed her eyes. "Their 2/4 time never wavers."

She blinked back her tears, contemplating what to do now. She had planned to tell Al about the baby when they were alone in bed later that night. She had found out last week, but she couldn't bring herself to tell him. She needed time to think things over, to get used to the new situation.

At first, she wasn't sure she wanted the baby, she wasn't sure she was glad, as everyone assumed married pregnant women were. She worried over her reaction and tried to separate her anxieties about being a good mother from her grief at losing her youth. Finally, she decided none of it mattered too much. The baby was coming. Women in dire straits might be able to consider the alternative of the back-alley surgeon, but certainly she never would. She would have to cope, a thought that finally satisfied her. She knew she was good at coping. Still, she postponed telling Al. She couldn't say why exactly.

She knew he would be excited, would have the usual responses of fathers-to-be. She imagined him picking her up by the waist, twirling her around, kissing her, then worrying that he had damaged the baby and setting her down gently, telling her to sit. He would never understand her uncertainty. Perhaps this was why she hesitated. But at work this afternoon, during a lag between typing assignments, she rushed to the bathroom to throw up. Swabbing her mouth with toilet paper, she decided she could wait no longer. It was time he knew. She would tell him tonight. Perhaps his excitement would be catching.

But now she felt thrown. What if his reaction wasn't so predictable? What if he decided he didn't want a baby now, that it would somehow curtail his affairs with other women? What if he fell in love with the sphinx-eyed woman?

After a few moments, not long enough for anything real to have happened with the dancer woman, Al returned to the table. He ran his palm over one of Evelyn's cheeks and smiled at her. He kissed her index finger. She was grateful his gesture of affection was in plain sight and Gloria and Edward couldn't miss it. At that moment, she knew he loved her as well as he could. Al love, incomplete, yes, but tangible. She would tell him tonight in bed.

The couples finished their drinks and parted, each having come in their own car. Evelyn opened the window. The evening was fair. One of the things she liked about Kansas City was that autumn was long and gradual unlike Chicago's sudden burning and dropping of leaves. Yet when she inhaled, she could smell a brittleness in the air that hinted at the coming winter. She realized she would be showing by Christmas and was pleased to find she liked the idea.

Their apartment wasn't far from the bar, but Al wanted to stop for cigarettes, so they went the longer way, which took them past a small newspaper kiosk that was open all night. Later Evelyn couldn't find any evidence that Al's drunkenness had impaired his driving ability. But obviously it had, for as Al accelerated through an intersection, another car hit them on the driver's side. It was Al's fault. He was killed instantly. Evelyn was fine, except for the miscarriage.

II.

Now Evelyn thought about that night on the twelve-hour train ride back to Chicago. She played the events over and over in her mind, trying to come up with a different ending, but she couldn't manage to make the Al in her mind accelerate later or earlier or decide at the last minute he didn't need cigarettes after all. Maybe by then the events were already fixed, so she went back earlier in the evening, to the jazz bar, to dinner. Then earlier in the day, earlier in the week. She kept going back—when they were first married, before the wedding, before they had even met. She traced her life back to when she was a child, looking for the one moment that might have altered this horrible outcome. But it was useless. She saw her life as the train on which she was riding, stuck on a track, unable to veer.

Looking out the window at the sheared fields and leafless trees, Evelyn realized how tired she was. Surprisingly, she had slept well since the accident two months ago, but she had been busy with arrangements of various sorts: first Al's funeral, then the move back to Chicago, packing and shipping all the things that had once belonged to her and Al, now hers alone. Each night's sleep had been hard and dreamless. Each morning, she had woken and begun the day's business before her thoughts could sprout. *Keep moving, keep moving.* This was the only refrain allowed to run through her mind. She even whispered it throughout the day as quietly as a nun in prayer.

Now, though she was still moving, she felt her body tremble with a weariness that she knew would keep her from sleeping. Anxiety and tension roped her muscles. She was glad to be seated, afraid the moment she stood, she would slump to the ground like a crushed shaft of wheat.

Success was unlikely, but Evelyn closed her eyes, hoping for obliteration. But instead, Al and the sphinx woman appeared. She opened her eyes and looked out the window to blur them away, but again and again she found them in the passing landscape as though they were burned into the soil. In the bare branches, she saw the cords of Al's neck as he leaned his face toward the woman, and the whole scene came alive in her mind: the disturbing music, the strong odor of smoke and the faint odor of urine, Al's bicep a hard ball as his hand pressed the woman's fleshy breast. "Oh, Al," she moaned.

The image was stronger than any other memory of Al her unwilling mind had formed so far. His hand, the woman's breast.

"Oh, no."

She didn't notice her own hand resting against her own breast, her fingertips pressing hard as if she might feel what Al felt, until the conductor announced the train's arrival at the Des Moines station. She was flustered and quickly pulled her hand away from her body. She clasped her purse, which was next to her on the seat, and picked up the small bag at her feet. She smoothed her hair with her fingers. *Keep moving.* She stood on weak legs and exited her car.

III.

There was a two-hour layover in Des Moines. Evelyn went into the station's diner. She began to salivate the moment she met the scents of coffee and bacon, yet she hesitated sitting down. For the first time in a long time, she felt awkward alone. Was her face smudged with her grief? *Keep moving.* Where to sit? She considered the empty booths, but they were large and unwelcoming. She wished she had thought to bring a magazine with her from the train.

She finally chose a seat at the counter next to a thin woman wearing dirty blue jeans and a tie-dyed tank top. Evelyn noticed her frail arms and wondered why the woman didn't seem to feel the cold weather outside and the rather chilly drafts in the coffee shop. In fact, she looked hot, her facial pores open and her skin shiny, as though she had recently been standing over the grill. The rusty shade of the woman's hair made Evelyn think of an old lawn clipper Al had left out one winter. By spring the blades had been ruined, but she had run her finger over them, enjoying the color of the residue against her skin.

Next to the woman sat a man with long, dirty blond hair, which was matted at the back of his head. An equally dirty bandana was wrapped around his forehead, and his khaki jacket had the sleeves ripped off. Printed on his bicep in puffy green letters was *Uncle Sam is The Man*. He wore sunglasses and smoked cigarettes between mouthfuls of eggs and bacon. Every so often, he leaned over and whispered something to the rusty-haired woman, who never replied with more than a small nod.

While looking at the menu, Evelyn noticed the woman's plate was heaped with food: scrambled eggs, fried potatoes, and what must surely be an extra-large rasher of bacon. The bacon, cut thick and fried to a crisp, looked good to Evelyn. She decided to order a rasher herself with eggs over easy.

When it was served, she ate with enthusiasm. She hadn't eaten much since the funeral, but now the pleasing textures of the eggs, just hard enough, and the crisp toast against her teeth and tongue made her jaw work quickly and constantly. Halfway through her meal, she ordered more bacon, unable to satiate her desire for salt. She drank cup after cup of the muddy coffee the waitress brought, lightly singeing her tongue again and again.

At one point Evelyn noticed the woman next to her watching her eat. She became embarrassed and instantly covered her mouth with her napkin as though she might hide all that she had consumed. But the woman smiled and nodded her approval.

"A woman should have a good appetite," she said when Evelyn had finally slowed her pace. "I hate to see them eat like birds."

"Yes, well, I was hungry," Evelyn said. "I didn't have anything before leaving this morning."

"You alone?"

Evelyn nodded. "I'm going back to Chicago," she said, then added, "going home," wondering if it were true.

The woman merely raised her eyebrows and nodded once again. Evelyn went back to her meal, but as she was finishing the last slice of bacon, unable to resist modestly licking her fingers, the woman leaned toward her, surprising Evelyn so she nearly spilled the coffee she was bringing to her mouth. She noticed a crumb of bacon and smudges of grease on the woman's cheeks.

"With that appetite, you shouldn't get back on that train," the woman whispered, her gaze shifting to the man next to her for a moment. Evelyn looked too and saw the man was concentrating on a book whose title she couldn't see.

"You should stay here and try the pie, try the lunch special," the woman said quietly.

Evelyn had still not replied, but she noticed the woman held her coffee mug close to her mouth, as if it provided the privacy of a curtain drawn around them.

"I think I've had enough," she said, embarrassed that she had made such a pig of herself and someone else had noticed. She felt the food bloating her now, making her drowsy, and she set down her coffee mug without drinking more.

The woman didn't register that she had heard Evelyn. She leaned back, considering Evelyn. Her eyes moved over Evelyn's body without guile, assessing her clothing and hair and all of the things Evelyn herself had looked at when considering the sphinx woman on the dance floor. She could feel this woman's gaze taking in small things, the shape of her ear, the way her muscles and veins twined in her arm. Evelyn said nothing and even moved to better accommodate the woman's gaze, interested to see what would materialize on the woman's face. Had Al's death scarred her body like the man's tattoo?

"Why are you going back to Chicago?" the woman said at last. The woman's voice was unnaturally light, and the smile on her lips tightened rather than relaxed her features.

Evelyn could see she was trying hard to sound casual, although she couldn't see why. Suspicious now, Evelyn considered ignoring the woman. But the question was one she was likely to be asked often. Her mother had warned her that friends and strangers alike would be curious. "Decide for yourself what you want people to know about your life." Her old life, she had wondered, or this new one thrust upon her.

"I'm moving back to Chicago to be with my family," she said, testing the feel of the words. "My husband—." Her breath caught. She hadn't had to say it so baldly yet.

Her mother had been told by the hospital staff. Everyone at the funeral had already known.

The woman's eyebrows arched with curiosity.

Evelyn steeled herself. If she didn't get the words out now, she might never be able to utter them. But her throat stuck.

"Go on," said the woman gently. "I'll take it with me to the grave. Let me."

Evelyn's shoulders slumped. She hadn't realized how heavy her grief had become. She wanted to moan. *How will I ever carry it?* She yearned for relief. And here was someone willing to bear the weight with her.

"My husband," she started again. "Al. He was killed in a car accident."

Now that the words were out, Evelyn felt calmer, as if her utterance had shown her what lay before her, with what she would have to cope.

But this, of course, wasn't everything. She had made sure only her mother had known everything. At the time, it seemed sensible. People were already distraught. Al's parents, Gloria and Edward, Al's friends from the factory. Their tears seemed to want something from her, something she couldn't give them. Their consoling sounds and touches burned her skin. But again and again, they forced their sorrow on her. This one thing, the baby she would never have, she had wanted for herself, and her mother hadn't disagreed, had barely mentioned it, and then only once.

But now Evelyn found herself wanting this woman to know the worst. She wanted something clean and complete. She wanted finally to give form to what had vanished before materializing.

She turned to the woman and said flatly, "I was pregnant. I lost the baby in the accident."

"Shit." The woman whistled softly, shaking her head. "That's a lot to lose at once." She lit a cigarette and tossed the match onto the few potatoes remaining on her plate. "Maybe you should get on that train."

Evelyn waited for the woman's reaction to run its course, as if she were watching a baking cake rise, then settle.

"No, women like you are essential. Really essential." She pounded the counter once with her fist. "Women who've felt things. Lost things."

Evelyn wasn't sure the woman was still talking to her. She seemed to be conversing with someone not in the room. She's crazy, Evelyn thought. Yet she liked that the woman's eyes didn't register pity, that she didn't move to embrace her or console her like all the others. Despite her distance, Evelyn felt the woman understood the heft of the words Evelyn had finally spoken, the effort it had taken Evelyn to hold onto them, then push them away. And it was done now. They were *out there,* beyond her. The baby, the miscarriage, they had moved from thought to reality in one moment.

"Listen," the woman said, locking her gaze to Evelyn's. "I mean it. Don't get on that train. Stay here." She looked to the man next to her, then back, and said so softly Evelyn could barely hear her, "Maybe I'll stay too?"

The woman's gaze now showed more shock than when Evelyn had told her of the accident. When she relaxed, her body seemed to curl in on itself like a caterpillar's. She pulled her coffee cup to her lips, then rested its brim against her forehead and closed her eyes.

The conversation seemed to be over, and Evelyn picked up the check the waitress had placed before her at some point. When she opened her purse, she felt the woman's hand at her wrist.

"Hey!" Evelyn said, pulling away, as if the woman wanted her money, but no hand went for her wallet. The fingers only gripped her wrist more tightly and even pulled her close. She resisted but only for a moment. Then she felt herself leaning in, only a little, but enough to smell the woman's scent, which was sharp like licorice.

"Sometimes the most unlikely choice is the only one to make," she said. Her fingers were cold against Evelyn's skin, but her cheeks were still red with heat. "Don't get back on the train."

She's crazy, Evelyn thought again. Yet she didn't appear to be. Evelyn looked at her more closely, trying to see beneath her surface. The woman's eyes were young, green but dark, dark as pine, Evelyn thought. Yet they were knowing more than crazy. But what was it, what did they know? Evelyn looked at the hand holding her and saw the fingernails were clipped short and had been scrubbed clean, but dark scabs stood out against the white knuckles as if her fist had been scraped against a brick wall.

Without a word the woman released her and leaned against the back of the stool. She unclasped the barrette that held her red hair. The strands dropped limply to her shoulders.

A hippie, Evelyn thought as she caressed the sore ring on her wrist, an unimpressive young woman in dirty jeans. Yet those eyes, they knew, they understood—what? Something. Maybe everything, and they wouldn't allow Evelyn to dismiss her. They made Evelyn want to lose herself there, as if in a thick forest.

The woman watched Evelyn watching her.

"So?" she said, not challenging but as if inviting her to share the softness of a featherbed, and Evelyn gave in, felt her whole body relax and fall. She had to hold on to the counter to keep herself on her stool.

"Sometimes I think the world is going to end," Evelyn whispered, amazed by her own words, but drunk with the sudden loss of tension. "Sometimes I think it should."

The woman smiled. "Yes, that's it. You've got it now. The world is ending, it's ended already." She stood, and the man next to her clapped his book shut and stood also, picking up a large duffle bag, which she realized had been on his lap the whole time. As the woman passed behind her, Evelyn felt that strong hand press and release her shoulder. The woman paused for a moment. "You're absolutely right," she said. "It's all over. To the grave." She crisscrossed her finger over her heart.

Then the man leaned in and said in a low voice, "You coming?" and she was gone.

Later Evelyn would not be able to pinpoint what, exactly, had made her linger in the coffee shop after the woman had left, after the train to Chicago had pulled out. Which words, specifically, had made her unable to move from her seat even as she was being called to board? Perhaps it wasn't words at all, she thought as she washed the grease off her hands and face in the bathroom sink, blotting them dry with toilet paper, but the possibility that she might have to endure the rusty-haired woman's gaze the entire trip.

She went to the ticket counter and asked when the next train to Chicago would be through. Three hours, the man told her, then another two for the layover. That wasn't so long, she decided. She would call her mother and tell her to come to the station later. She would read magazines and watch the television in the waiting area. After all, there was no hurry. What, really, was waiting for her at home?

She was watching a rerun of *I Love Lucy* when the show was interrupted for a breaking news report. A bombing. Although terrible, this wasn't so unusual. There had been plenty of bombings lately. Evelyn didn't know when or why it had become such a popular form of protest, but it had. This bomb, however, had exploded on her train, on the one she didn't take. Already twenty people were reported dead. There were likely to be more.

Evelyn breathed heavily, first unable to get enough air into her lungs, then, having gotten too much, the world seemed to dissolve for a moment, go black. She thought she might faint.

The world is ending, the world has already ended.

The footage of the bodies being removed from the wreckage was blurred and confused. Her head ached as she watched what she realized from the sudden shifts must be a handheld camera. But she couldn't turn away. At one point she thought she saw the woman from the diner, but she couldn't be sure from only the smudge of red hair.

Evelyn again held tightly to her purse as if it might steady her. It could have been me, she thought.

The air in the station was suddenly too thick, filled with smoke and grease from the diner and the scents of too many bodies. She still felt she might faint, so she walked out of the station and stood on the platform, the chill air stinging her nostrils. She huffed to see her steamy breath shoot from her lungs as she had done when she was a child. She walked up the platform, listening to the clamp of her heels on the wooden slats beneath her. The wood was worn, sagging in the places people most often stood and soggy where water trailed down from the roof, collecting in puddles which she carefully stepped over. *It could have been me.*

Three tracks away the engine was being hooked up to the passenger and freight cars. An elderly man with gray hair and a paunch balanced on the end of the engine as it moved slowly down the track. It would be so easy, she thought, for him to slip, or jump. The possibility of collision was everywhere now. Even at this slow pace, she realized, such a fall might be deadly. Bloody images from the television appeared and disappeared in a flash. But the old man held on with confidence, looking beyond the train and the station into the field of overgrown grasses that poked through the thin layer of snow. When he neared the other cars, he stuck out his hand and caught them as if reaching for the reins of a horse that might suddenly bolt away. He fiddled with levers and heavy chains and waved to a man on the ground, who in turn waved to someone she couldn't see. The train, now connected, began moving slowly, and the gray-haired man continued to balance. Once again, he looked beyond himself, into the field or at nothing at all. *It would be so easy.* She stepped closer to the edge of the platform, which was now vibrating under her feet, and looked down the track. She saw the headlight of an oncoming train. The vibrations increased, and she felt shivering in her ankle joints, up her calves, and into her knees. She pressed her hand against her heart and felt the movement of her chest. "Easy," she said aloud, but covered her mouth, although nothing could be heard over the sound of the train, which was now close and didn't look to be slowing.

When she reached the platform's edge, she stepped into air, just for a moment, just long enough to feel her muscles go limp as they had in the diner, as if expecting to be caught. But they wouldn't give in for long before refusing and tightening. Unbidden, her fingers grasped for and found the cold metal of the lamppost, and everything in her body screamed at her that it was too late. *Too late!*

Only her shoe dropped as the train hit. The shoe ricocheted back onto the platform, its heel shattered. She continued to hold fast to the post as the train rushed past her, lifting her hair from her neck and drying her eyes. She forced her lids open, letting the current coax more water from her ducts. She smeared the water over her cheeks as a caboose the color of late-autumn cornfields passed.

Back in the station, she rejoined the few other passengers. In her stocking feet, her ruined shoe in one hand, the undamaged one in the other, she watched the small screen. The bodies were still being taken out of the train, laid on the soil next to the tracks. The people seemed so small, the bleeding arms and faces so captivating they might have been painted by some Old Master. It was like nothing else she had ever seen. Not like her own accident at all. Not Al's broken face. Not her thighs smeared in blood. That pain was hers. This pain. Nothing.

After a while her eyes burned so hot, she looked away. She found a seat near a window, far from the television. She sat down to wait. Waiting was all that was left. It was everything now. Of course, it would be longer than expected for the next train due in. And it would have to take a circuitous course. She would be on board, carried home after all, the route only being longer and feeling endless.

Bush League

Lake Milfoil's water level had dropped to record lows. I stood on the footbridge, watching Remy Lawson's crane fish a mud-caked Trans Am from Milfoil's grubby depths. Parrot feather and coontail, greedy at the best of times, had choked out the pike, leaving them bloated and belly-up. Word was, kids messing around among fish carcasses dove down and found Tram, as we used to call Morris's ride.

The summer's heat had been relentless. I lifted my face to the sky, and the sun pricked my cheeks like hot knives. Sweat trickled over my ribs, down my belly, pooling at the waistband of my jean shorts. For months, it seemed to me the whole of Privy had been walking with chins lifted, lips parted like the beaks of baby birds, hoping mother sky would drop cold rain down their gullets. Dry, scratchy, they swallowed hard and moved syrupy slow. I swallowed hard against the putrid odor of the dead sand pike that rose with the crane's limb.

Could be a hundred shit cars down there, I reassured myself as a rusty bumper broke Milfoil's surface. Then that damn spoiler spoiled my hope. A collective *oh!* rose from the crowd. I pushed my shoulders back so no one would see I'd winced at the car dangling from the crane's hook like a prize bass.

"Morris," I whispered, only now realizing I hadn't really believed it was him, not in my bones. Would his bones still be strapped into the driver's seat? He never wore a seatbelt cruising the back roads for whole nights, and I wondered what went through his mind as he readied himself for the shortest drive of his life.

After eight years, would my emerald clutch purse still be on Tram's backseat? Would its contents have survived? Sometimes in my dreams, I tore through alley garbage cans searching for that purse. All I ever set dream hands on was oozy dreck. Please, please, let it all be oozy dreck now.

I couldn't take it and looked away, toward the paper birch forest along the opposite shore, to the boulder where we all used to build bonfires, drink crap booze, and listen to the classic rock Morris loved. Usually when I crossed the bridge, I memory-heard his voice, crisp as a cold beer, strumming his bare belly and hum-singing Steely Dan, "Kid Charlemagne" and "My Old School."

"Oh, no, Guadala-hmm, hmmm, won't hmmmm . . ."

No doubt, the boy could croon.

He loved to peel the paper bark from those white trunks, baring the pink flesh beneath. "You're skinning those trees alive," I said once. He left the birches alone after that, only stripping fallen branches.

That was Morris. He never meant to be cruel.

For the first time, I didn't expect to see him on that rock and forced my gaze back to the river.

Inching onto the flatbed, Tram shimmied and drooled mud. Was he there? I couldn't see. Maybe he wasn't. Maybe he faked his own death, or in this case, double-bluffed it the way he used to with pitchers when he was stealing bases, shuffling out and back and out again.

I pressed my forearms into the spot on my belly where he liked to grab my fat roll and pinch. He'd have a lot more to pinch now. Eight years on, did *his* bones have any flesh left to pinch?

Much as I needed to know, I didn't want to see.

I walked off the footbridge, gaze on my sneakers, refusing to look at the other gawkers. A few people called my name and reached out to tap my shoulder as I weaved through what could be considered a pretty good crowd for a nothing town like Privy. Don't touch me, I thought. But I forced myself not to wince again. Get them on the scent, and it's all over. Just ask Morris.

At Nunzio's people were already talking about the car. I longed to slip in the back door and get my hands into some dough before anyone could speak a word to me, but I forced myself through the customer entrance as usual. The shift from the scalding noonday sun to the frigid pizza-scented darkness of Nunzio's made me woozy. I teetered at the cash register for a moment, eyes closed, listening to the pinging of the old pinball machine and Rosa's teeth working her spearmint gum. Shut your damn mouth when you chew, I wanted to shout at her. You're no baseball player. You're no Morris MacGregor, pacing the dugout, wrapping and rewrapping your fingers around a bat. He had a piranha grip. My hand went to my belly again remembering purple bruises. Then my stomach roiled and my lungs heaved, desperate for air.

"Bet it's Roderick's heap," said a voice scratched raw from cigars. "He got a wad of insurance payout when they claimed it stolen. For real, who'd steal that hunk o' junk?"

"Nah, I know for a fact it ain't Roderick's," said another voice. I kept my eyes shut tight, but I recognized the lisp as Tommy Lane's.

"How you know, Tommy? You got something to confess?" That was the voice of Preacher. He hadn't seen the inside of a church in thirty years.

"Never you mind, Preacher. I ain't no loose lips. Besides, we all know that's Morris's vehicle." He pronounced it *vee-hickle* as if he were some backwoods Southern yokel and not just a normal old Privy yokel. "Spoiler will tell. I helped him put on that spoiler myself."

"You okay, Elly?" Rosa said softly, interrupting herself mid-chaw.

I opened my eyes. Enough of Nunzio's regulars stared that I knew I'd better play it cool. "I need a Coke," I said. "It's the Mojave out there today."

I must've stood there too long without moving because Rosa shoved me with her elbow as if I were crowding her. It wasn't hard to make it look convincing. Like mine, her shape was closer to pie round than breadstick narrow. Her clay-red hair was cut short and stood in spikes. She charcoaled the rims of her eyes into neat lines, but today the heat smeared the kohl to storm clouds.

"What, Elly?" Rosa said. "You need GPS to get to the soda fountain? Get your drink and get on the line. We got pie orders backed up like Route 43 during harvest fair."

I could have hugged her. Nothing was more normal at Nunzio's than a pileup of pie orders at lunchtime. I filled a red plastic cup with crushed ice and Coke and headed for the kitchen. Damn, if Rikki didn't start right in before I had tied on my apron.

She pulled her mouth to the side in what she probably thought was some kind of old-timey gangster whisper but wasn't a whisper at all. "Did you see him? Is he in there?"

I shrugged. I took the ball of dough she'd been kneading and let it droop over my knuckles. Made me think of the slime drooling from Tram. "We got orders," I snapped, flicking my wrists to get the dough spinning. I wasn't going to let her drag me into anything here, but she looked so sad, her frown all hound dog, that I added, "Later." I flicked my wrists harder, twirling the dough in the air. "We'll go to Trawlers after closing and talk."

"Yeah," she nodded knowingly. "Ears have big pitchers."

"Something like that," I said.

She kept staring at me, so I flipped the dough her way, and out of instinct, she caught it on her knuckles. She spun it back into the air and halfway up to the ceiling. I smiled. Rikki still had great hands. She went farther in Little League baseball than most boys. Despite her bag-of-bones frame, she'd been a powerful hitter. And she could bullet a ball home from deep in the outfield too. In Little League, she'd given Morris a run for his money. In high school, she'd had to settle for softball. She never could make the transition to fielding and hitting the bigger orb. "Feels like I'm knocking a pumpkin head off a scarecrow," she'd say, spitting into the dirt Dand kicking her own saliva every time she popped one up for an easy out. So she lost any chances for a college scholarship or playing pro that she might have had if she could have stayed with boys ball as she said on repeat whenever she had too many drinks.

I'd been an average hitter and fielder, softball and hard. In a larger town, I'd have ridden the bench if I'd made the team at all. My talent was scouting. I liked to ride around the state and watch other teams play, analyzing form, calculating attitude, and making predictions on the upcoming season. Still do ride around looking, although not as much what with the hours I put in tossing pies. Rosa had long ago insisted I abstain from Nunzio's baseball pool-for-pies contest so the customers could win instead.

Rikki tossed the dough again. I snatched it out of the air, dropped it onto a pan, and swirled sauce over it. I said softly, "I couldn't tell much of anything."

"It doesn't feel real," she said. On the field Rikki liked to keep her cap pulled low, the brim and her lank dishwater hair hiding any tells she couldn't control. But at Nunzio's she pulled her hair into a high ponytail, revealing milk chocolate puppy eyes. She turned them on me now.

"It's not right," she said. "Never was."

"Not here." I shook my head.

She nodded, and I nodded, and we got on with clearing the pie jam. We'd barely made a dent when she wiped her hands and untied her apron. "I have to see." She slammed out the back door, her sneakers scraping gravel, presumably headed toward the scene at Lake Milfoil.

I cleared three orders before she returned.

"Well?" I said.

Silently she retied her apron as Rosa called from the front, "Sheriff's man just phoned in a tall order for pickup. He'll be here in twenty."

Rikki gasped. I narrowed my eyes at her. "Not a word," I said.

I held her gaze with mine until she nodded. Could I trust her? Rikki was skittish, but she was tough. So were her pies that day because she pounded dough as if she were wearing in a new mitt.

I was back at the soda fountain, filling up on Coke and ice again, when Roger pulled in to pick up the order. I sighed with relief. Of course Sheriff Dougan would send the lowest head on the deputy line to bring back lunch. Roger was only a year out of community college and still had the shiny, over-clean skin that made him look under-cooked.

Rosa took over before the regulars could start grilling the kid.

"Pull the cruiser up to the door off the kitchen, Rog," she said before he'd gotten halfway inside. "A stack of pies is way easier to load out there."

"Yup." He headed back out the door.

Right there was the reason we'd voted Rosa manager, her masterful way of nudging things in the right direction without anyone knowing they'd been nudged. Cleaning and wait staff worked hard for her. She worked our money hard too, investing back into the place when we wanted to play with some of the dough we made.

Largely because of her, all three of us now made a decent living, decent enough for Privy anyway. There wasn't much to spend money on unless you were part of Privy's crescent moon of richie-riches like Morris's family.

Morris's father, Billy MacGregor, brought in the chain stores that choked up Highway 57 and choked out the local stores in Privy. With times so hard, Mr. MacGregor had bought family homes around Lake Milfoil for spit. He bull-dozed the modest cottages and built luxury condos and mansions, selling them to outsiders. No one really knew much about the people who lived in them or how they managed to pay for all their grand stuff. If we bothered to feel anything for them, we felt sorry. Those richie-riches had swimming pools they had to hire Privians to clean, granite floors to polish, paintings and statues to dust, grounds to groom. Rosa, Rikki, and I were like most Priv-ians, satisfied with a couch, a decent TV, and a stocked fridge.

Rikki's job at Nunzio's was to fill in where needed. She liked being a floater. She waited tables, made pies, or manned the register. Floating meant she could take off on a bender for a few days without notice. She'd firecracker around town, spitting sparks, leaving trails of smoke, knowing we'd always come looking for her and lead her back to one of our couches. Drying out, she looked raw and ashamed. We never asked, but if she felt like it, she told us what she'd done, confident we'd keep it to our-selves. We were some of the best secret-keepers in the world. If there were trophies given for keeping secrets, Nunzio's would have a wall stacked floor to ceiling with gold-plated first places. As it was, we only had a couple of plastic seconds and thirds for bowling.

I was in charge of keeping the kitchen stocked and in order. I used my scouting knack to find suppliers and hag-gled for closeout ingredients for near nothing. Sure, sometimes we served the worst pies on the planet until the deal-of-a-lifetime stock ran out. The candied yam pizza never caught on. The fish ball pies reeked of throw-up. But sometimes I jacked it out of the park. The sardine-and-green-pepper became such a favorite we got a picture and write-up in the county paper. We framed and hung them on the wall opposite the bowling trophies. Rikki in the middle, Rosa and me on either side of her. A strange shadow lingered next to me. Whenever I looked at the picture, I thought, there's Morris, hanging out with his favorite girls.

I've had years to perfect my order-and-inventory system, ever since we bought the place from Carlita Nunzio, using the money we'd found in the duffle bag, buried spot-on where Morris told us he dug the hole: seven birches to the right of the boulder. No one would ever find that duffle with Mr. MacGregor's initials embroidered into it. After we bought Nunzio's, all three of us crammed into Rosa's Chevy truck and drove south, over the state line, to the Ossage landfill. We dumped wreckage from the restaurant's renovation: crumbling drywall, rotting studs, blasted-out trim. Among torn window shades and scarred flooring planks, the duffle bag had been another toss off, gone for good. Too bad Morris and Tram didn't have such a decisive ending.

After closing that night, Rosa and I slid into a back-wall booth at Trawlers. Normally Trawlers had the best air conditioning next to Nunzio's. Tonight all ventilation seemed blocked.

"It stinks," I said, wrinkling my nose as if sniffing old catch, ten days ripe. "We should go someplace else."

Rosa threw me a disgusted look that said I knew damn well there was nowhere else to go in Privy besides Nunzio's and Trawlers. We'd have to drive up the highway to one of Billy MacGregor's chain joints and sip girlie drinks like cosmos or mojitos. *Shoot me now*, her eyes said, although her red hair spikes were already drooping.

Derrick, Trawlers's owner, had decked the walls and ceilings with parts of fishing boats: poling platforms, bent gunwales, sidelights sparkling here and there. Cockpit seats lined the bar, with cleats screwed in to hook your jackets on, not that anyone was wearing one in this heat. A weirdo sculpture made of wrenched Bimini tops and cracked propellers that looked like they came off a homemade spaceship was usually my favorite bit of décor, but tonight the violent metal felt like a warning.

Most of the parts came from richie-rich boats that crashed due to newbie handling or excessive drinking. Would Derrick try to get a hold of Morris's waterlogged Tram? I wondered. Of course, Morris hadn't been inept or in a drunken accident. An accident is when you don't mean for something to happen, but it does. Goddamn *nothing* about Morris plunging into that brown water lacked intention.

Pounding from the ceiling speakers was some country-rock-hip-hop mess that couldn't decide what it wanted to be. There was a decent crowd but still plenty of room to move. Rosa poured beer from a plastic pitcher into frosted mugs. She slid one over to my side of the table.

"It stinks," I repeated, "and it's hot."

"Heat must be straining the system," said Rosa. "Have a beer. You'll cool down."

"Where's Rikki?"

"Ordering shots."

"I don't want any. I'm already spinning."

"They aren't for you. Or me."

"She's bending," I said. It wasn't a question but a confirmation.

"Seems like it. Think she'll keep it together?"

I scowled and leaned over the table. "She's been squirrely all day," I said. "Nearly as many ingredients landed on the floor as on dough. She never misses. And she made me tune in that classic rock station Morris liked." I sat back. "Jesus, nothing but Journey and Steely Dan all day long. Even this bullshit music is a relief."

"Think we should do something?"

"Not sure what we can do."

We drank silently. A moment later, Rosa gestured with her chin toward the bar. I fake stretched and followed her direction. Sheriff Dougan sauntered toward Rikki.

"We can keep *him* guessing," Rosa said, her voice low.

"Yeah," I said. "*We* can. Can she?"

We exchanged doubtful looks.

"Shoot," I said, rubbing sweat off my glass. "She's got as much to lose as we do. She's just letting off steam."

"Yeah, maybe," Rosa said. "Should I go get her?"

"Give it another minute. She'll keep her mouth shut."

But I wasn't so sure, and by the time Sheriff Dougan steered her toward us, his big paw curled around her bicep, I was downright unsure. The sheriff was twice the width of Rikki, which made her twice as skinny. Soaked with sweat, his black pompadour flopped in strings over his forehead like an upturned mop. When he forced his lips to smile, the skin around his eyes sprouted deep creases, maybe from squinting at too much human craziness. Rosa and I both liked Sheriff Dougan. He made sure a cruiser circled at closing time when Nunzio's regulars might be hesitant to give up their tables for the night. I felt bad we couldn't be straight with him.

"She lined up five shots and sucked them boom, boom, boom," he said, jangling Rikki's arm. "She'll need someone to watch her tonight."

"We'll take care of her," I said, getting up so Rikki could slide in and use the wall for support. "Like always."

"Don't worry, we got her." Rosa nodded. "We won't let her drive. I'm designated. One beer and done. Scout's honor." She raised two fingers.

Below his sweaty mop-strands, Sheriff Dougan's expression showed skepticism. "Girl Scouts' salute is three fingers. My Janie's leader of her troop."

"I only made Brownie," Rosa said. "Pledge counts just the same."

"Listen," he said, dragging a chair from a table and mounting it horseman style. "You gals hear we pulled that MacGregor boy's car out of Milfoil today?"

Of course, every pie eater in Privy had felt it their sworn duty to tell us all day long.

"We heard," Rosa understated.

I watched her to see if her eyes would skip to Rikki, but she kept her gaze steady.

"Would it surprise you to learn Morris MacGregor was strapped into the driver's seat?"

"That is a surprise," Rosa said without hesitation.

"Yeah," I said, backing her up. "Morris told us he was pulling a Kerouac. We thought that meant going on the road, not off the dock." It wasn't a complete lie. Morris had always wanted to road trip. To my relief, Rikki was slumped and drooling in the corner. I said to Rosa, "Did Jack Kerouac drive into a lake? I always mix up those bad boys, James Dean, Jim Morrison, Freddie Prinz."

"Janis Joplin," said Rosa.

"She's not a boy," I said.

"Jimi Hendrix then."

"Superman," Sheriff Dougan offered.

"Superman?" Rosa said.

"The actor who played Superman in those old television shows died in a hotel room under suspicious circumstances."

"I thought that was the guy from *Hogan's Heroes,*" Rosa said.

"Him too," Sheriff Dougan said.

"There you go," I said. "Happens all the time."

"Maybe, but Morris MacGregor wasn't any war hero," Sheriff Dougan said. "He wasn't any Superman either."

Rikki, not passed out after all, suddenly piped up. "But he liked shots." She melted into a sloppy wreck of sniggering laughter.

"What's that?" said Sheriff Dougan, cupping his ear.

"Don't mind her," Rosa said. "She's tight. Four tequilas, you said."

"I said five. What's that, Rikki? About Morris?"

Her eyes were closed, but her lips parted as if to say something. Before she could sink us all, I lobster-pinched her thigh, just above the knee where I knew it would hurt most. She yelped, clamped her mouth shut, and snored unconvincingly.

"Guess she's asleep," I said.

"Listen, you gals got a nice little thing going at that pie place."

"That's twice you called us *gals*, Sheriff," I said. "Surely we're more than that now."

"Business women," said Rosa. "Entrepreneurs, at least."

"I always wondered how you got the seed money," he said.

"A generous uncle," Rosa said.

"I know all your uncles. Played ball with most of them. Not one could keep a dime in his pocket past payday."

"A penny-conscious aunt?" I offered.

"I'm not joking," he said. "A boy is dead." He paused for a moment before adding, "A rich boy whose daddy may want a few answers. You all were his friends. Or so everyone says."

"We were his best friends," I said.

"So if you have something to say, you say it now."

"And if we don't?" I said.

"Say it now?" he said.

I nodded.

"Then be ready to keep your peace to the grave." He stood, scudding back the chair. "All of you." He pushed his chin in Rikki's direction.

She looked genuinely asleep now, and I thought how heavy her dead weight would be dragging her to Rosa's truck and into my apartment.

"By the way," he said. "We found a green purse in the back seat. Scummy but salvageable."

Rosa lifted a leather sack the size of a saddlebag. "I got mine here."

"Don't carry one," I said. "I just slide a wallet into my jeans pocket."

I noticed he'd given up on Rikki and addressed Rosa and me. He pulled a folded sheet of paper from his breast pocket. It was damp at the edges from sweat, and he had a hard time peeling it open.

"Either of you recognize this?"

He held a photograph of the purse that had once been the perfect complement to my dress. We had agreed to go to prom as four stags, no dates, but we all looked good. Morris wore a tux he'd found in his grandfather's attic wardrobe. In the picture, my once-pretty purse was ugly, the buckle rusted, the vinyl cracked and scummy as Sheriff had said. I'd given it to Morris after prom because he liked it so much. When would I ever wear that dress again and need a matching purse? Morris was a peeler, and as with the birch trees and every beer bottle he'd ever fisted, he'd gouged the vinyl surface although without piercing it. I only remembered his nail biting in as I saw my old purse now.

"Never seen anything like it," I said, not so much to Sheriff Dougan or Rosa or even passed-out Rikki, but to the universe that pinched its very own piranha grip on my throat.

#

For weeks, the local newspaper nursed every damn detail of the investigation, speculating why Morris was naked, using some cooked-up math to estimate how fast he'd accelerated off the dock to get that far out, doing a history of Trans Ams. Lon Angus, who'd come home from the state university with a journalism degree, came by Nunzio's, acting happy to relive old times. Took me and Rosa two seconds to sniff out he wanted background on Morris. Rosa pushed him out the door with this month's special in hand: a Vienna-sausage-and-chick-pea calzone.

I was glad Rikki hadn't been there when Lon came pawing around. She was in bad shape. She came to Morris's funeral service reeking of booze. The cops had gotten all there was to get from Morris's remains, so they turned him over to his parents to burn and bury. A bronze-colored urn and Morris's senior-year picture had been placed on a pedestal. People popped open umbrellas to cast shade during the sunbaked service and used the "Dust in the Wind" song sheet as a fan. Still, plenty looked like they were ready to pass out. A full bench of Morris's baseball team showed up, looking uncomfortable in their grown men's bodies, sweat patching their dress shirts.

We placed ourselves smack dab in the middle of the gathering. Rikki had gotten so far down the neck of a bottle she could barely balance on her seat. She whimpered, and I was afraid she would start wailing like a Baptist. There was no point in telling her to keep it together though, so Rosa clamped Rikki's face against her breasts, which pillowed out of the scoop neckline of her dress.

"I never thought. Not really," Rikki slobbered into Rosa's boob.

"Shut her up. Sheriff's right there," I hissed quietly. After a moment, I added, "We owe Morris some respect."

Rosa nodded. "Shhh, now," she cooed, patting Rikki's hair. "Let's just tell Morris goodbye. Properly this time."

She managed to keep Rikki from disrupting the service. Afterward, we didn't manage to avoid Sheriff Dougan. He cornered us heading to Rosa's truck. He'd combed his hair back. A few stubborn strands drooped over his damp forehead. His uniform shirt clung to his chest.

"She all right?" he said, finger-gunning at Rikki.

"Grief stricken," Rosa said. "We all are."

"Looks stricken by something," he said. "Funny thing about grief—"

"Doesn't seem funny to me," I said. "Not today, Sheriff. Not one little bit."

"Funny thing about it," he said, "is that grief looks so much like guilt."

I saw Rikki's head lift from Rosa's chest and eye the sheriff. Her nose had globs of mucus clouding the nostrils.

"Thought you were going to let things lie," I said quietly.

"I never said that. Or if I did, that was before Billy MacGregor made a stink about wanting some answers like I thought he might." He cocked his head and dipped low so he could capture Rikki's gaze. "Blessed thing about confession, Rikki, it's a perfect balm. Soothes the mind."

"Leave us alone, why don't you?" I said.

"Soothes the soul," he said. "Like slipping into cool water."

"You're doing this *now*?" I spat at him.

"Look around you. Life's short," he said, his gaze still on Rikki.

Dripping with sweat and anger, I was about to give him a good goddamn piece of my mind when Rosa said, her voice soft as a breeze, "The thing about cool water, Sheriff, it turns cold come autumn and turns to ice come winter. So then where are you? Winds change real fast. We sure don't want to be caught out in a blizzard." She smiled and half-pulled Rikki away. I smiled too. No one could mix a metaphor like Rosa, and Sheriff should have known better than to go one on one with her.

"C'mon, sweetie," Rosa said to Rikki. "Let's get you home and into a bath. Sheriff's right, a bath is the most soothing thing in the world."

After Morris's funeral, the thermometer stayed red, and so did Rikki's eyes. Gone for days at a time, Rosa and I would catch a whiff of her here and there and chase her down. Late one night at Trawlers, I caught her and Tommy Lane doing it over the toilet in the women's bathroom, all drippy and nasty, fluids trailing down their limbs. I dragged her back to my place and pushed her into the shower, dousing her with melon-scented shampoo. A few days later, Preacher told us he'd seen her stumbling along the highway, wearing one shoe. He said she threw rocks at his car when he stopped to offer her a lift. "Gal's still got an arm," he said. "Took out my taillight."

Rosa gave him a free calzone and thirty bucks to get his light fixed. She told him to keep his mouth shut about Rikki, that we'd take care of her. He nodded, tucking the cash in his pocket and stuffing so much calzone in his mouth, he had a fifty-fifty shot at chewing or choking.

When he left, Rosa stood at the pass-through window. "We gotta do something."

I agreed, and we left the hired hands to run Nunzio's. We drove the county looking for Rikki. Always seemed we were a hair's breadth too late. She'd just left Trawlers. Just bought a twelve-pack at Zimm's. Just been kicked off of the high school's baseball field after peeing on home plate. Finally, we went to the boulder. We hadn't been there since Morris drove off the dock and we dug up the money he left for us.

She wasn't there, but we weren't sure where else to go. I fingered the scar on the birch where that fateful night Morris had stabbed his rambling note to its trunk. He pleaded with us to tell his parents he'd taken their money to go on the road, Kerouac style. *Don't tell them playing baseball was too hard. Forget me. Don't tell them anything else. Please, please. Don't tell them I'm a cheat, a fake, a nothing. Use the money so they think I took it for my trip. Have good lives. Please don't laugh at me.*

Pissed me off, then and now, that Morris thought we would laugh at him. A cheat though, that line was grayer. He never played sly tricks like some others, never greased his cap visor with Vaseline or corked his bat. So maybe he bowed under the pressure a bit, but there was no deviousness in it. Like pinching me and stripping those birches, Morris never meant to hurt anyone. The boy just wanted to be free. And intention matters, right? This last question is the one that kept knuckle-spinning in my mind as we tracked Rikki.

Fact is, Morris's being gone hadn't bothered me as much when he was *in* Milfoil as it did now that he was buried in that urn. Before, I let myself believe he was out there, driving Tram every which way. But the idea of him stuck in that ugly-ass urn for eternity hurt. And now, despite all his intentions, he was taking down Rikki too.

I clambered up the boulder and screamed at the muddy water, "Baseball's just baseball. Goddamn it, Morris. No freaking reason to go driving into Lake Milfoil."

The last time I saw him alive, we hadn't even bothered with clothes, skinny-dipping in Milfoil. Rosa and I took her father's truck to get more beer while he and Rikki kept swimming. When he wasn't looking, I'd tossed my purse onto Tram's back seat, saying, "There you go, Morris. That's for you." After, when I read his shame-filled note, my fear for him as deep as that knife stuck in the birch, I wondered if he thought my purse was some way of laughing at him.

As Rosa and I drove away, I heard him call after us, "What you think I need a purse for, Elly? You saying I'm—?"

We were gone, radio blasting, before he finished that sentence, and I've spent eight years finishing it for him.

When we got back with the beer that night, Morris and Rikki, and Tram too, were gone. We figured the mosquitos drove them off, and after slapping the buggers off ourselves, we drove home too. The next day, the three of us found the note, the money, and the skid marks on the dock. Rikki swore she didn't know what happened while we were gone to make Morris do such a crazy thing.

I prayed for Morris's forgiveness every time I passed Milfoil, apologizing for that purse, promising we'd honor his wishes to the last. And we did. We played along, saying we thought he'd gone road tripping. We used the money well. And we never once called the boy a cheat or laughed at his expense.

I wouldn't go back on that honor promise now, no matter what overwrought iron bar Rikki was twisting herself into.

"She's been here," Rosa said.

I jumped down from the boulder. Empty bottles of her favorite beer were laid out like heat-stroked players on a field. A few embers still smoked in the ring of rocks that marked the bonfire pit. I shoveled a few handfuls of dirt to fully douse the embers. We drove for hours, refusing to give up on finding her that night, finally limping home defeated but hoping she'd shown up on one of our couches. She hadn't.

The next afternoon, Rikki turned up at Nunzio's. I felt sore looking at her bloated face. "Must be a summer flu," she said, dumping a scuttle of dirty dishes into the sink for the dishwasher to deal with. She hadn't bothered to put on an apron, and I noticed ashy streaks fingered across the belly of her powder-blue tank top.

I pointed to the marks. "You been starting fires at the boulder?"

She shrugged. "Something like that."

"Such dry heat, Smokey Bear wouldn't be happy," I said.

"Fuck Smokey. Fuck you too."

The dishwasher who'd been covering her shift while she boozed and screwed all over town looked sideways at us, his eyebrows raised. Enough was enough, I thought. I grabbed her arm in the same place Sheriff Dougan had. With my two inches and forty pounds of inventory-hauling weight on her, I quick-stepped her skinny, hungover ass into the walk-in fridge. I slammed the door behind us. Despite our upset, we both inhaled with pleasure at the slap of cold air.

"What's wrong with you?" I said.

Her eyes narrowed, going from hangdog to attack dog. "You're kidding, right?"

"You've got to pull it together. I know it's been weird since they pulled out—"

"I'm dying of thirst," she said. "We got any juice in here?"

"Since they pulled out Morris."

"Morris! He loved his juice," she said, curling over and laughing.

"That's not funny!"

"No?" she said, bolting upright. She stepped close and gave me the look she used to toss a pitcher when she wanted to intimidate. But I was no stranger from another team. I knew her as well as I knew anyone in the world. I stood my ground.

She didn't step off either. In the wintery air, her hot breath clouded my cheeks. The smell was funky with yeast and vomit.

"You thought it was pretty funny that first time you gave Morris those pills," she said, her voice hard, her eyes narrowed.

"What pills?" I said. "What are you talking about?"

"Oh, right. The honor code. We don't talk about Morris unless we're praising the mound he threw on. Glory be to Morris's golden arm!"

"Who told you I gave him pills?" I said. "Not Morris?"

"He said you just wanted to help him out of his slump. That you'd heard big leaguers do the same thing, and he had scouts coming to watch him play."

"I never gave him pills." But then it came to me. "Wait, that's not true. I gave him—"

"You all like to forget how bad he got. That last day, he was so wrecked he could barely hit my powder-puff throws much less a real pitch."

"I remember."

"Yeah, well, you ruined him. You're no better than a dealer doling out the first hit of free meth."

"That's not true," I said. "I gave vitamins. That's all."

I'd bought him a jar of Flintstones chewables. He laughed so hard he snorted beer out of his nose. "Elly, babe, you are one crazy girl." Then he swallowed a handful. He claimed Wilma tasted best.

"What does it matter now?" I said.

"Everyone thought he was so great," Rikki spat. "Such a *great* ball player. And he was, until you ruined him." She leaned against the wall exhaustedly. "I'm telling his parents. They should be glad their cheating freak son is dead."

"You can't do that to Morris."

"Morris, bullshit. You just don't want to give up this shitty restaurant. We should never have taken that money."

"It's what he wanted."

She said nothing. She was so hot, steam rose from her skin.

"Honestly," I said. "I never gave Morris anything but vitamins. Kids strength. Flintstones."

She still said nothing but clenched her face and puffed breath hard through her nose.

"Okay, tell them," I said finally. "We lose this place. What then?"

"He stole that money. His dad may be a shit, but we had no right."

"We did what Morris wanted."

"Morris was a cheater. A thief and a cheater."

"Why do you keep saying that? You know, I never understood why he called himself a cheater. And you always got so squirrely when I asked you about it. But you tell me now, Rikki."

"The second he swallowed the first pill, he was done. It was over. By the end, he was shooting those steroids into his toes."

"What? Steroids?"

"You never noticed how bad his skin got? How his temper flared? Said it helped his nerves. No worse than a shot of whiskey before a game, he claimed."

"Shit," I whispered.

"Yeah."

"But I never gave him those, Rikki. Did he actually say I gave them to him?"

She hesitated. "No. I just saw you hand him a bottle once."

"The Flintstones. That's all I ever gave him. I swear. But even still. So he took those pills. He was messed up. But who cares? He was still Morris."

"I cared!" she spat, leaping forward and knocking balls of dry mozzarella to the floor. She kicked the cheese into the corners. "I told him so too."

"What do you mean?"

"That night, before he drove off of the pier, I told him I loved him."

"What?"

"Elly, you think you're so smart. You never knew anything. He *loved* me."

"Did he—?" I asked.

"He wanted me to go away with him. To take the money he stole from his father's safe and pull a Kerouac, just like he said in the note."

"So why didn't you?" I pictured Morris and Rikki out there in the world. Driving from town to town. Spending his father's money. Why *couldn't* that have been true? Who knows what Rosa and I would be doing for money, but at least Morris would be alive. "Why didn't you both leave?"

"I had one condition. He had to quit the pills. Quit everything."

She was pacing now, but the fridge was so small she could only take three steps before turning around. After a few turns, she grabbed her forehead as if she were dizzy. Her hands shook. She punched her left bicep with her right fist.

"Stop it," I said. I knew her better than anyone, and I didn't know a thing about her. I stilled her fist and held out a brick of hard butter.

She took the butter brick and tossed it hand to hand. "But it had gone too far. It wasn't just steroids by then. I never thought it would go so far."

"What do you mean?"

"He'd started doing other things too, Adderall and crank . . ." She worked the butter, which despite the cold air was warming in her hands. "He was . . . I never thought."

I didn't respond.

"It wasn't fair that he was going to get to try out and maybe play ball for a real team. It should have been me." She'd softened the butter, forming it into a ball with her strong hands. "I had the stuff to go pro too. I'd have given anything just to play triple-A. Worked my ass off. My nerves were rocks."

It was true. Back then, nothing had been able to shake her.

"But Morris. Fucking Morris, talent, sure, but not a salt grain of mental toughness. That night after prom, I told him—"

"What?"

"The truth. When he wouldn't agree to quit the drugs, I told him he was a cheat. He didn't deserve me or to play ball. I told him I was going to tell everyone what a blue-balled cheater he was."

"You didn't."

"You know what he had the fucking nerve to say?"

I didn't respond. I watched her hands shift the butter hand to hand.

"Said my talent was all in my head. Said Coach told him me being a girl had nothing to do with me being cut. Said my timing had gone so far off Coach claimed I'd never get it back. Which was crap!"

Her breath was heavy now.

"After all I'd done for him," she continued. "Driving all the way to Jackson to meet the guy. Making sure no one could connect him to those vials."

"You bought drugs for him?"

"I just wanted him to win. If he won, it was a little bit like I was winning too. I didn't think . . . I never thought . . ."

Shocked, I stood silently, my body suddenly icy with sweat.

"And then he goes and says that I'm a nothing? A loser? Because I won't run off with a cheater. No, worse, a cheater and a thief and a *quitter.*"

"Oh, Rikki, no," I whispered.

"So I told him just what I thought of him." She bent over suddenly, her torso shaking. I thought she was crying, but when she straightened up, I saw she was laughing. She cackled so hard tears splashed her cheeks. She sucked air and squeaked, "And I told him to do everyone a favor. 'Go fucking drown yourself,' I said. And I meant it!"

"No," I whispered.

"The cheating, thieving, goddamn cowardly fuck!"

I stared at her twisted red-rubber face that barely resembled a human, that barely resembled anything.

"And he *did* it, the goddamn fuck." She laughed and laughed, spit drooling from her mouth and nose.

I'd seen her a thousand shades of ugly, but never like this. My stomach roiled with disgust. Morris, he never meant to hurt, but Rikki had known exactly what she was doing. And I'd been making excuses and covering for her all this time.

"It was you all along," I said. "You knew this whole time and never said a word."

She stopped laughing and stood tall, shoulders wide, eyes narrowed to a challenge. "You always think you're so much better than me, Elly. You and Rosa. But you two took his money quick enough. You built this place on his back. Made a cozy little life for yourselves."

"You helped him cheat," I said. "You told him to kill himself."

"He was a big boy. Made decisions all on his own."

Something else suddenly occurred to me. "Shit, it wasn't just the steroids you helped him get. It was your Adderall, wasn't it? I always wondered why you stopped taking it. Now I know what you meant when you said you worried you'd end up like Morris."

"Fuck you!" she snapped. In one move, she shifted her weight and thrust the butter ball full force at me. But all the booze and years had slowed her. I ducked, and the butter ball slapped the metal door and broke into bits.

Rikki pushed past me and tore out of the fridge, disappearing out the kitchen's back door.

#

Rikki's next bender took her round the bend. She didn't come to Nunzio's, didn't pretend to be sick.

"We should go look for her," Rosa said. She'd just finished closing out the register, and I was wiping down the back.

I shook my head no.

"Take a drive out to Milfoil?"

"No point," I said, rinsing out the rag.

"Why not?"

"She's already gone," I said. "She left with Morris."

Rosa studied me a moment before nodding and tapping a beer for each of us.

As I turned off the lights in the kitchen and went to join Rosa at one of the tables, I wondered how much she knew about that night Morris killed himself. We'd never talked about why Morris drove into Milfoil. Foolishly, I'd thought my purse had pushed him off the dock. Did Rosa have her own guilt secreted away?

"Did Rikki tell you?" I started, but Rosa stopped me flat.

"We owe them both the same," she said.

Do we? Hadn't Rikki's cruelty released us from obligation to her?

"We take their secrets to the grave," she said.

I hesitated, not sure this was right, but it was all that was left.

"Okay," I said.

We sipped our beers in silence.

#

Days later, Tommy Lane kicked into Nunzio's to shout out the fire down by Lake Milfoil.

"Right where Morris MacGregor took his swan dive."

"Near the boulder," I said.

"Burned the dock and two of them new houses Billy MacGregor built. So far. Still raging bad. More shit-luck for the MacGregor family."

"Guess so," said Rosa softly, her gaze steady on me.

I got busy filling orders.

Rosa and I stayed at Nunzio's that night, waiting for Sheriff Dougan to come by as we knew he would. We'd been drinking beer for hours but couldn't catch a buzz, so we switched to soda. We cleaned the whole place, scrubbing baseboards, washing windows, pulling down the picture of the three of us in the newspaper to wipe the walls. We were contemplating whether to hang it back up when Sheriff Dougan arrived.

Leaning against the counter, he stooped like a tree that just couldn't fight the wind any longer. A film of soot coated his skin and clothes.

"Have a seat. Coffee or coke?" I asked.

"Coke," he said, sitting at the table with Rosa and me. He reeked of smoke and exhaustion. He drained two full glasses before he spoke.

"Found her against that big boulder. You know the one?"

"We know," said Rosa.

"Acres have been lost. No telling how much damage before it's all over. She had no idea what she started."

"I tried to warn her," I said.

Rosa gave me a sharp look.

"Said it was too dry for fires."

Sheriff chewed some ice and watched us eye each other.

"For the last time, you gals got anything you need to tell me?"

"For the last time, we're not *gals*," Rosa said, turning her gaze on him, releasing us both.

"Not for a long time," I said.

He sat thoughtfully for a moment.

"Billy MacGregor wants someone's scalp," he said. "At least an explanation."

"Billy MacGregor doesn't get everything he wants," Rosa said, setting down her glass with surprising force.

"Not this summer anyway," said Sheriff Dougan. He swiped a napkin over his face. The white paper came away streaked black. "I'm going to have to tell the man and his wife something."

"You know what, Sheriff, tell them a love story," I said. "People eat that shit up."

"What love story?"

"You got a boy and a girl, a lake and a ball field," I said. "Surely there's a love story in there somewhere."

After a silent moment, he stood. He picked up a trophy, studied it, and set it down again. He swallowed the last of his soda. "Time to head back," he said. He paused in the doorway.

"She doesn't have much in the way of family," he said.

"We'll take care of it," Rosa said.

"Yeah," I added. "We're designated."

#

It took all night to put out the fire. Likely it replaced Morris as the main topic of conversation everywhere but at Nunzio's, where the regulars knew better than to bring it up. At our place, the chatter circled the World Series. Most years, when the talk got passionate, I would be right in there, ignoring stats and win-loss records. I looked for the best fusion of players. But I'd lost my taste for the game. Seemed to me, winning only meant someone else was losing. Mostly I stayed in the kitchen, playing solitaire, letting the hired hands make regular pies. I hadn't the heart for a special this month either.

When the time came, Rosa and I had what remained of Rikki's remains cremated. Fighting fire with fire, Rosa said. We talked about keeping her urn at Nunzio's alongside the bowling trophies, but we had to admit, she'd never loved the place the way we did, and she hardly liked bowling at all. If Rosa thought of burying Rikki's urn next to Morris's, she didn't say so to me.

Instead, with Rikki in the truck between us for the last time, we drove past Lake Milfoil and the charred ruins without stopping. The heat had broken, and a cool wind hissed through the bare branches of the few trees that had made it through the fire. By spring there'd be new growth, but it wouldn't be the paper-skinned birches Morris loved. Only the scrub would survive.

We sprinkled Rikki's ashes over the high school's outfield. I stood on the home plate she'd pissed on and batted a few balls toward her, but I was out of practice and barely hit beyond the bases. Rosa and I sat in the grass with her, passing a bottle of her favorite beer back and forth.

Afterwards, as Rosa pulled her truck onto Route 43, heading back to Nunzio's, I squinted hard against the bright sun. I wished I could imagine Morris's car disappearing over the hill, with Rikki in the passenger seat, arm out the window and waving. Why couldn't that have been true? I squinted harder at the burned-out forest and Milfoil's drying bed. As we drove farther away though, finally reaching trees untouched by fire, I leaned out the window so the wind could slap my face. I stayed there for the rest of the ride, listening hard for the rustle of leaves that resembled the scuffle of the crowd in the stands. I very nearly heard it.

Sleight of Hand

I

Last night I dreamed of a bat. I don't think it was a real bat. No. Not like bats really are. But it was a real bat in my dream. It was fuzzy. Thick and fuzzy and fast. It hung above me, feet clutching the ceiling fan, wings extended like a shawl, tongue rubbing its black nose as it swung around the room.

After three rotations, the wings drew in like two webbed Slinkys. It loosed its grip on the fan, dropped like a bullet. Wings shot out, and it caught itself midair. Springing and recoiling, springing, recoiling, it swooped. Came close to my hair. Darted away. Dipped low and brushed my bare leg with one cold, fleshy tip as thin as crepe paper.

I awoke from this dream with a start so violent I pinched a nerve in my neck. The twinge ran all the way to my fingertips. I thought the dream bat bit me, so I tried to lie very still, to find the bat fluttering in the blank room. The pain eased, and gray shadows emerged. I could trace the familiar outlines of the swing neck lamp, the brass clothes rack, the jacket hung over the edge of the door. I reached out to where you usually sleep, used to sleep. My fingers, expecting your warm skin, brushed cold sheets and recoiled like the dream bat's wings.

II

I've never liked the Van Gogh print you insisted we hang in the kitchen above the automatic drip coffee maker. *Sunflowers* you called it, pointing out brushstrokes that were supposed to indicate genius. One morning I followed your finger with my gaze, noting that, indeed, there were brushstrokes, but I still didn't like the colors. Burnt orange, harvest gold, sienna—the colors of autumn.

Still, *Sunflowers* greeted me every morning as I waited, bleary-eyed, sometimes hungover, for the coffee to drip. Knowing *Sunflowers* would be there became a kind of comfort. Each morning I listened to you shuffle about getting ready for work: drying your hair, gathering props, warming up your fingers by tossing a tennis ball from hand to hand.

"Morning's the best time to catch the working stiffs," you told me, kissing me high on my cheek. "They're still half asleep . . ." You rubbed your hands together like a mad scientist. "*Suckers!*"

I knew how they felt. With you they hadn't a chance.

It was morning when we met, and I was vulnerable. Just a cup of coffee and a subway ride into my day, you appeared in the train station, juggling four, five, six tennis balls. Like a cat watching a fly, I was mesmerized by the sunny orbs. When the platform cleared of commuters, you caught the balls one after another, and they disappeared into your giant leather bag. I rifled the bottom of my briefcase for some change. All I came up with was a package of Alka-Seltzer and a miniature Bic lighter. I dropped them into your coffee can, certain you'd be offended by my paltry offering, but I wanted to give you something. You took them out and stuffed them into the pocket of your jeans, saying, "Thanks. I got a headache, and I need a smoke." Winking, you pulled a gold coin from my ear and pressed it into my palm. After you were gone, I saw it was tinfoil and chocolate and your phone number taped to one side.

I'm still vulnerable in the morning. *Sunflowers* doesn't help. After studying it impatiently for years to the burps of brewing coffee, I thought I knew the strokes so well I could duplicate them myself. Last week I went into the art room at work and asked the artists to let me paint for a while. I pictured the strokes I knew so well. My mind wrapped around the textures and shapes, saw the sunflowers in all their sad beauty, but my fingers refused to make them true. When I finished, my picture was nothing like *Sunflowers*. My watercolor strokes were runny, loose, not lush like Van Gogh's oil, and my flower looked like something from a *Star Trek* episode. But the colors were the same overripe hues as in the Van Gogh. I brought my painting home, taped it to the refrigerator, and titled it *The Announcement*.

Now, each morning, I stare at *The Announcement* instead of *Sunflowers,* knowing, as usual, I should have paid more attention to your hands.

III

Gindy and I spend the morning in Ennui. Crystallized strands of snow whip across Roger's Park and past the cafe's window. Pouring granules of brown sugar into my coffee from an envelope the color of grocery bags, I watch cars cut through the snow, scattering the strands. Through the opposite window, I watch the whitecaps of Lake Michigan crash against the breakwaters. The ones that make it over regurgitate pebbles and sand and trash onto the shore.

Gindy reads articles from *The Reader* aloud, noticeably avoiding the ones involving death.

"Look," she says, pointing to a couple cuddling hands. "Bet they slept together for the first time last night."

"Beats sleeping alone."

Her eyes widen as she remembers you. "Jesus, I'm sorry."

"It's okay," I say, although, of course, it's not. But I know it's not her fault. Everyone tells me it's nobody's fault.

To ease her embarrassment, I tell her about the first time you and I came to Ennui. We had just signed the lease on our first apartment together and were eager to explore our new neighborhood. It was summer, sticky and thick and hot enough to swim in the lake. White plastic tables and chairs were scattered on the sidewalk outside the cafe, and four men the color of our coffees sat at the table next to us.

We toasted to our find: hardwood floors, French wrought iron windows, a half-block walk to the lake. The men at the next table shouted and gesticulated and touched each other in a language we could not understand. We wondered if they were arguing or if this was just the way they talked, and I had to hold your wrists to keep you from going over and asking them to settle our debate.

I told Gindy that we spent as much time away from the apartment as possible that first year after we discovered the closed wrought iron windows sang a perfect and pure high "A" when the wind was off the lake, which, of course, it nearly always was. The sound was maddening. When it was hot, we chose mosquitos over monotone and left the screenless windows open all night. But in winter, tormented by the shrill wail, we lay awake, touching toes and thighs and stomachs. Once you matched your voice to the sound, harmonizing sweetly for one long, loud breath.

Later we moved, just five blocks away. But the silence was disconcerting, and we couldn't see the lake.

The apartment is always silent now. I don't turn on the television anymore. The sound of voices filtered through wires is eerie. What if I mistake one for yours? You were always throwing your voice, behind a couch or into the refrigerator, surprising me with a thin falsetto in my soup or a husky growl on my hat until I learned to expect you everywhere. Even if you weren't in sight.

Now there's only silence, except there is really no such thing as silence in Chicago. But I hear things I never heard before. Through the closed storm windows sneak the grindings of garbage trucks in the alley, snatches of conversations, throbbings of rap music. On Sundays, gospel sounds float from across the hallway, and I can hear Dora singing along with Reverend Bill.

"LORD, LIFT ME UP! Oh, lift me up. LORD, LIFT ME UP! Oh, lift me up."

She's tone deaf but enthusiastic. I picture her jowls shivering with blissful devotion as she dances from room to room, dusting or sweeping. When I saw her in the elevator, I complimented her on her strong voice.

"I ain't religious," she said. "I just like the music."

You listened to music for four days straight after we came home from the clinic, one positive, one negative. You didn't sleep, although you didn't move from the couch either. After playing every record, cassette, and compact disc in the apartment, from Sex Pistols to Charlie Parker, you ordered Chinese food. Twirling the bamboo chopsticks between your fingers like batons, you said, "I want you to be ready. When the time finally comes, I don't want to worry that you'll be shocked."

"C'mon, I don't want to think about that. It's like giving up."

"Being ready isn't giving up."

"I don't want to think about it, okay? Besides there are all kinds of drugs now . . ." I picked up a spring roll soaked with oyster sauce and tried to put it in your mouth.

"*For Christ's sake . . .*" You grabbed it from me and threw it back onto the plate. "You never even try to see things. Right in front of you. You never even fucking *look!*"

For two years you dropped death into our conversations. You were ruthless in your desire to make me look behind the curtain. You talked of sickness, joking that this was one way to finally lose the extra pounds you'd been carrying around since puberty. You scowled if I flinched and came up with more and more grotesque images—emaciated bodies, open sores, uncontrollable bowels. You read me articles about modern leper colonies during dinner and the resurgence of leech bleeding over coffee. Finally, like your voice, I learned to expect illness anywhere, everywhere.

But I kept my faith. New things were being discovered every day. When I heard scientists had discovered the gluey substance that holds an atom together, my faith was bolstered. If they could find that, then surely they would find something for you in time.

It was nice to have something to believe in. It was something I hadn't felt since Sister Ruthilia, my second-grade teacher, prepared our class to receive the Eucharist. We were fourteen children about to enter the fold. In music class we practiced all of the First Communion favorites: "Take Our Bread" and "Praise God From Whom All Blessings Flow" and, because it was the early seventies, "Day By Day" from the musical *Godspell*. All fourteen of us—except for Tom Fuller who had flunked first grade and knew already he was destined for the darker side—took our upcoming initiation very seriously. Sister said we needed ready hearts if we wanted to receive the Lord in them, and I prayed intensely and minded my mother for weeks to prepare mine.

The Sunday finally came, and I listened to my new shoes, real dress shoes, delighted by their sliding and scratching as I tapped across the glossy marble church floor. Left-together, right-together. Like tiny married couples, we processed in twos down the aisle. I gave the first reading: "Little children, let us love in deed and in truth and not merely talk about it . . ."

When I finished, I glanced at my parents, and my father gave me a small nod, and I believed I was on the verge of holiness. From now on, wherever I went, I would be illuminated from behind like the church statues of St. Veronica with her shroud and St. Stephen with his arrow-punctured chest.

Later, as I knelt for the consecration, my weight crushing my knees against the wooden kneeler, I looked at the blood-dripping Jesus hanging on the cross, and I gloried in my own painful knees and tried to press myself harder into the wood.

Finally, it was time to receive the host, the flat white wafer that would fill me with God and light. All the children stood up together. One by one we slid out of the pew, genuflected, and stepped up to the priest. We had ten seconds—Sister Ruthilia had timed us on her great silver watch—from the time our knees hit the floor to the time we said *Amen*. Ten seconds and I would be filled with the Holy Spirit. I would never again feel pain. I would love and mind my parents always. As though I was swallowing a potion, I would suddenly, and forever, be glorious and glowing.

On my way back to the pew, I salivated and tried not to chew the body of Christ. I let the host dissolve on my tongue, waiting for the aura to encircle me. I tried to pray, but I couldn't help sneaking glimpses of my new halo. I couldn't see anything though. It must be like trying not to meet my own eyes in the mirror, I thought. So I concentrated on my prayers—Hail Marys and the Act of Contrition I had learned for first confession—careful not to break the spell. But my stomach growled from fasting. My skin itched under my lace collar. The wood hurt my knees even more, and the wafer left a sour taste in my mouth. But I kept the faith, certain all I needed was a mirror to help me see. After pictures and brunch, I rushed not to the kids bathrooms, but the grown-up single one where I could stare as long as I liked without fear of others looking on.

I closed the door, flicked the light switch, and looked in the mirror.

There it was! The light shone all around my head, just as Sister Ruthilia said it would. Suddenly, my light was gone. All light was gone, and I was bathed in blackness.

In my anticipation, I had forgotten to lock the door. I hadn't seen Tom Fuller ease it open and flick the light switch off. I didn't hear him lock the door until it was too late. I heard his familiar cackle on the other side, clear as the church bell.

I cried hot tears in the dark, angry at Tom Fuller, disappointed by my insufficient light, afraid I had not been ready for a real halo, or that I had been ready for nothing at all.

IV

We never detect the right signs because our eyes are always trained elsewhere, straining to see clearly. We look to the horizon when our own feet are making footprints or at the ground when it's the sky that's raining. And there's no one to tell us where to look—even visionaries wear blinders sometimes.

When you became sick, you insisted we see a lawyer. "I want to think about you with the time I have left," you said, "not legal bullshit."

I hated you for giving up and for knowing all the ins and outs and for being so goddamn *right*. As I kissed your dry lips, I felt the warmth of your breath and remembered every death mask you had painted for me. Yet I refused to brace myself, and it turned out you got well.

There was victory in my relief.

V

Two days before you left, I came home from work to find you perched yoga-style on the couch, staring at the plum and the apple and the kiwi gathered in the hole of your lap.

"Shot," you said. "They're fucking shot."

"What?"

You picked up the plum and the apple with one hand and the kiwi with the other as I had seen you do hundreds of times before with whole bowls of fruit or boxes of tools or cabinets of toilet paper rolls. You tossed the plum. It carved a shadow into the lamplight, reaching its apex just as I thought it would hit the ceiling. As it dropped, you tossed the kiwi, the plum landing with a thwack in your palm before you released the apple . . . thwack-kiwi— thwack-apple—thwack-plum-thwack-thwack-thwack thwack-thwack-thwack-

thwackthwackthwackthwackthwack . . . your hands receiving fruit sure as a surgeon's receiving instruments.

"See?" you said, catching all three.

"What?" I insisted.

"My timing," you said as though exasperated with a child. "It's SHOT."

I couldn't see a thing except your beautiful hands.

The last time I saw you, you were airborne and heading into the horizon, as they say, to visit your parents. You took presents. Not the ones you usually buy for your family at the expensive Magnificent Mile shops. We couldn't afford those anymore. This time you took pieces of yourself to leave behind:

–Sister: the records you'd collected since you were twelve (including your Carpenters dark phase)

–Mother: the walking stick from Ireland that you sanded and stained yourself

–Father (the hardest, you said): a framed picture of you and him, arms wrapped around each other's waists, taken on your twelfth birthday

"Bring me back a souvenir," I called after you as you headed to security.

You waggled a small pink snake of a tongue at me until the traveler behind you gave you a shove to get you toward the plane.

VI

Normalcy is pliable. It moves as we move, adjusting itself to our lives. I picture you airborne now, floating, so I guess it makes sense that gravity seems to have gotten weaker, that the world seems more loosely connected than it used to be. Things as solid as the oak dining table, which took four of us to lug up the steep, winding steps of the brownstone, now feel vapid.

Roaming the apartment one day, I climbed atop the table. I took off my shoes and socks, trying to feel the wood solidly beneath me and the floor solidly beneath the cabriole's clawed feet. My own pale feet looked like two fish served up on the smooth, hard surface that you or I had oiled once a week for years. I slid the toes of one foot across the table. Slippery, yet I couldn't quite feel it against my skin; it might not have been there at all.

Still, it is the ordinariness of life that is shocking, more shocking, even, than listening to your mother, whose voice broke as she told me about the pools of blood staining the concrete of the highway.

"The only one," she said, choking on the words, "the only one—one in the whole pileup—five cars—that was even seriously hurt."

"Oh, God," was all I could think to say.

"It should have been me," she said finally, sniffing thickly. "My car was behind . . . I don't know what made me swerve at the last second."

"Reflex," I said.

"Yes, I just reacted. Just in time."

I saw it now, your timing. Shot.

Somehow, I work, I run, I sleep, eat, wash underwear, pay bills, and wait for the impact, ready to wince. But it never comes.

VII

Onetwothreefourfivesixseveneightnine. Ten seconds. A ten-second phone call, and nothing will ever be the same.

At work today, I write the same travel brochures over and over: "Say 'Hej' to Sweden!" "Say 'Aloha' to Oahu!" "Say 'Hola' to Acapulco!" I pace after completing each brochure. Carpeted partitions split the office like ice cube trays, the tap-tapping of computer keys coming from each. Opal's nasal voice is more agitated than usual, so I avoid the corral, the horseshoe of conference tables stacked with papers, files, and half-eaten remains of takeout food. I hide in my cube and read back issues of *Condé Nast*.

I pour over a spread on London's Covent Garden. Once a fruit and vegetable market like the ones still tucked into the winding streets of SoHo, Covent Garden is now a pricey tourist attraction with hand-painted clothing, wooden marionettes, and fanciful jewelry. There are street performers too: scriveners and saxophonists and magicians like you. There is a half-page photo of a woman in flight. Her body, in its sequined leotard and ballet shoes, is tucked into a ball and is being catapulted onto the waiting shoulders of her partner. The caption reads, "Without mats to cushion a fall, the tumblers' timing must be perfect."

Drinking thick coffee, the dregs of the last morning pot, I picture you there, juggling fiery torches as you'd always wanted to do on the streets of Chicago but couldn't because of fire codes. I see your saffron streaks in the gray sky.

#

After lunch Opal summons me to the corral to order me to rewrite Georgia-Pacific's Monte Carlo campaign. As she bellows, already in a frenzy from dealing with the airlines, her pale cheeks bounce, and her fleshy pink lips wriggle like two worms mating.

"They won't want this." She throws the dummy brochure at me. "You know their campaign's on a schedule. What were you thinking?"

I watch her fleshy folds jiggle in anger. The fluorescent light engulfs her brassy hair.

"Saffron streaks of fire," I whisper.

"What are you saying?"

It's then I understand. It doesn't matter where you look. It doesn't matter how bright the light. You'll never see it all. Not when you need to, before maybe, or after, but not when you need to see it.

"Why are you saying anything at all?" she continues. "I don't want to hear anything except you'll get the damn campaign done perfectly and on time."

"You stupid woman," I snap, blind now with anger and understanding. "There's no such thing as perfect timing."

She bawls something, but I no longer hear her voice. I only feel my body shaking, creasing, convulsing. Tears stream down my cheeks. I lose my balance, land on the soft green carpet, and roll halfway under someone's desk. When I look up, Opal stands above me, staring, the worms of her mouth curled into a misshapen O. Her face, fuzzy above her lip and on her chin, reminds me of the dream bat. I scream and hit my head on the underside of the desk.

VIII

Opal insisted I go home. I was glad to leave and not be fired. But I haven't gone home. Instead, I walk to Lake Michigan, eyes on my feet to shield my face from the wind. I am surprised to find the beach empty. It seems there is no one in this huge city for miles. The air is frigid, but the breeze from the lake is warm. Water retains the heat of summer all winter. I know this only because of you.

"It's called the lake effect," you said, delighted by nature's illusion that what keeps us warm is icy water.

"You know you've just spoiled it for me," I said when you insisted on telling me how they cut the lady in half.

"If you'd just open your eyes," you said, leaving the ending hanging.

I wonder now what you thought I'd see. Whatever it was, I know that you were wrong. It doesn't matter how closely you look; what's behind the curtain is only another curtain, behind the sunflowers only canvas, another covering. And looking behind only misses the point.

Snow falls in thick flakes. I lift my face to the steely clouds and watch the snow rushing toward me like falling stars. The flakes dissolve on my cheeks and in the frosted water, and I watch my breath disintegrate into nothing, into everything.

Breakneck

After weeks of drought, curtains of cold rain drop onto the hot blacktop of the parking lot, surrounding the Oakland Beach house. Lena Granger stands on the deck at the back of her apartment and breathes in the grimy steam. She wishes she were gazing at an ocean view as the beach name suggests, but she's in the scrappy part of town, the ocean two miles away. The beach itself is plenty scrappy in its own right. It's shell pocked and gravelly, strewn with broken beer bottles itching to cut your heels and toes. Harley lowriders cram the beach's parking lot. Halter tops and bared beer bellies expose hides leathered by years of hanging out in exactly the same place every summer.

Whenever she and Jeremiah walk there to catch a breeze off the water, those lowriders seem to barely notice their own babies, tiny sausage fingers picking up fishtails and horseshoe crab carcasses, loose diapers dangling into the frothy waves from their dirty asses. Bad parents, she used to think.

Not that she'll be a good parent either, she admits now, thrusting a hand out to test the intensity of the rain, which feels less like a curtain and more like water balloons exploding in her palm.

Jeremiah will be a terrific father though. No question. His excitement at a chord change in a pop song sends him spinning. His hand on her waist, he spins her too. He'll twirl their baby in the rain. They'll make mud patties and sing songs together, and not that Barney crap either. Real songs about love and hope.

If she has the baby.

If Jeremiah reappears.

Behind the house, instead of a beach, a weedy field sprawls. Its surface has cracked like the skin of an overripe tomato, so the rain cuts streams into the hard soil. The streams lead to a line of birch and chokecherry trees. Beyond that, the highway's octopus limbs lead into and, more importantly to her, out of the city.

If she could hop on one of those highway tentacles, she'd be safe.

She chews her thumbnail, a habit Jeremiah hates. She'd give anything to hear him chide her, to feel him wrap his fingers around her hand and ease the thumb from her mouth. She'd douse her nail tips in chili pepper to quit the habit if they could hop on that highway together and race out of town.

This is only one of the many deals she has offered the universe in the past two days. The universe or the devil. *Bring him back, make it all okay, and I'll . . . or I'll . . . or I'll . . . I promise.*

She sidles toward the corner of the house, looks without turning her head, and confirms that the Mercedes SUV is still parked a few houses up the street.

"Shit," she says softly.

Its dove gray color screams, "Don't notice me!" But what could be more noticeable than a Mercedes in this neighborhood of hooptie Taurus station wagons and crumbling work trucks? For a while, in the spirit of Jeremiah, she dared to hope the stink of this area—a blend of hot dogs, rotting lettuce, and excrement that's always more intense after a rain—might drive the Mercedes' occupants off. No such luck.

"Game on," Jeremiah had said when he brought home the suitcase, which is now shoved beneath their bed. And that's exactly how he'd treated the situation, as some sort of game. As if they'd finally be winners.

Lena glances through the bedroom window at the bed she hasn't slept in much since he vanished two days ago. She shifts her gaze back to the Mercedes. "Jesus Christ, baby, this is no goddamn game," she says. "Brought home a suitcase full of serious shit. And where the fuck *are* you?"

She calculates how fast she can run from here to the path severing the tree line. She might make it if she goes breakneck. She ran cross-country in high school and won a race or two. Sneakers or, given the mud, hiking boots? No, they pawned her boots to make last month's rent. Sneakers are faster anyway. But even in sneakers, can fear outrun wrath? Can desperation beat greed or—she doesn't want to think it—revenge?

Greed had been the starting pistol to this race. At the time, it hadn't felt so much like greed. But then she hadn't known greed could feel like the first wisps of moisture cutting through fevered air. Or a soft layer of new snow. Or Jeremiah's fingertips trailing down her back. She'd thought greed meant wanting gold chains, diamonds, a rapper life-style, or maybe a Newport-mansion life.

All she and Jeremiah wanted—want, she corrects her-self, *want*—is one more fresh start.

She knows now this reasonableness is the wizardry of greed. It wraps itself in the lifestyle you think you deserve, the one you expected before the bad luck and the mistakes and the regular shit of life sucked you down shin deep, then chin deep.

She inches farther along the balcony, confirming that Jeremiah's Ranger is still parked there too. The name on the truck makes her heart hurt. Jeremiah had stenciled the letters in black paint, *LENA* and a *G* next to the truck's name: *LENAGRanger.* She wasn't sure she liked her name out there for everyone to see, but Jeremiah said it made him drive more safely, knowing she could be crushed to bits.

"Should have thought of that before you brought that fucking suitcase home," she whispers. Immediately she pleads, "Please, please," as if the truck could bring Jere-miah back.

The Ranger is her other option for escape, although surely the moment she backs it out of the lot, the SUV will be on her tail. The truck's normally dull burgundy paint has turned glossy in the rain. You wouldn't know it has a tricky starter, an oil leak, and a shot glass of gas in the tank.

Goddamn if deception isn't everywhere. She promises the universe, here and now, if she and Jeremiah make it out of this mess okay, she'll live ugly. She'll *be* Lena Granger: disappointment to her parents, a bag of bones and unfulfilled potential, a loser with no luck and no reason to hope for better.

She shinnies back to the open screen door and slips inside the apartment. She hasn't left since Jeremiah vanished except for these forays onto the balcony. It's hotter inside. Stinks more too. The air conditioner broke three weeks ago. They'd been planning to go to a big-box store, get a new one when the suitcase paid off, but . . .

Lena plugs her nose and heads for the unwashed dishes swarming the kitchen sink and countertop. Despite the nose plug, she gags. Yesterday, going crazy each hour, each minute Jeremiah didn't come back or call, she'd struck another bargain with the universe: drink every drop of liquid, soil all the cookware, smear every plate, glass, and piece of cutlery, including the set of Schlitz beer mugs from Jeremiah's grandfather and the Boleslawiec au gratin dish from her great-grandmother. Then Jeremiah will reappear.

It's been harder than she thought. She pours the last shot of Jim Beam into the belly of an ice cream scoop and ladles the liquid down, burning her throat. One drink doesn't hurt the fetus; all the books say that. She drops the empty bottle and the scoop into a bowl of congealing tomato sauce in the sink.

She sits down at her light table and tries to work.

The photographs for the sporting goods shoot are due this evening, and she's nearly finished. She can't blow off the shoot despite the circumstances, maybe especially because of them. If she can finish the job, they'll deposit money in her account. Not really enough to run but enough for a start.

With or without the suitcase? With or without Jeremiah?

She can't see that far ahead.

The irony is that she's the photographer, but she counts on Jeremiah to have vision. At the beach, he's the one who spots the smoky plumes of an osprey high in the clouded sky. He separates the charcoal skins of migrating seals from the flint-colored rocks they loll on. He sees flowers and trees and birds she registers only as swirls of color.

Because of Jeremiah's vision, they'd come to Rhode Island where he swore there was a scene and a whole world of natural beauty just beyond the concrete. She'd find plenty of work. He'd restart his landscaping business.

But they'd found Rhode Island to be an exhausted sigh, a seedy state with a seedy soul. At least what they could afford of it. The lavishness of the Newport mansions he showed her annoyed her. No one should have so much. He tried to show her what he saw. "Look at the gardens," he said. Vibrant flowers, hedges jetting to the sky, grass greener than any field of alfalfa on her parents' farm. "People like us make that beauty," he said. "It exists because of us."

Besides, he insisted, he didn't bring her here for Newport. "We just want a little bit more," he said. More space, more time, a little wiggle room, a little fun. He turned her toward the ocean where waves rushed and exploded over rocks.

"Look," he said. "Can't you see us? We're floating. We're flying."

The navy water and the powder sky filled her, but the thin line of the horizon kept her unsettled.

"Just a little bit more," he repeated.

Little Bit. She closes her eyes and hears him whisper the words, his lips petting her belly. *Little bit.*

For Little Bit, he took the suitcase and brought it home.

For Little Bit, he shot his shot.

Little Bit is why she knows he hasn't left her.

He's been taken from her.

What she doesn't know is why. Not exactly. The characters watching from behind the darkened windows of the Mercedes haven't come in and taken the suitcase. What are they waiting for? What do they want from her?

She bends over her light box, her stomach churning from the whiskey and past-its-use-by-date tahini she'd finger-licked from the jar earlier. She tries to focus. She hasn't done a nondigital shoot in a long time, so she's out of practice working with real film. She presses her eye to the 10x loupe, assessing the three shots she'd taken of a fishing vest.

A moment later, a crash on the street sends her leaping from her chair. Hands shaking, she finds herself at the front window without memory of having moved her feet. She hugs the wall and peers through the natural part between the fabric and the window frame. She can't risk rustling the curtains. Focusing her gaze through this sliver of light is not unlike looking through the 10x loupe, which she dropped when she jumped up. Both require an amount of tunnel vision.

The crash had been the Riccis' blind Labrador nosing the trash bins. But at the end of the vision tunnel, just beyond the driveway of Spike's Junkyard Dogs, looms that goddamn Mercedes. A gray hawk. Scanning for prey.

The Labrador trots off with a moldy looking wiener in its jaws. Lena's stomach roils. Normally she doesn't mind the smell of Spike's. And the night Jeremiah disappeared, they hadn't wanted to heat up the apartment by cooking, so Jeremiah offered to go get dinner. She'd been working on the shoot. "You stay," Jeremiah said. "It's my turn to fly."

What if she had been the one to go out, she thinks, pressing her chest against the stucco wall and studying the SUV. Guilt and fear roll down her ribcage with her sweat.

"Come on," she whispers fiercely to the gray car. "Just come already. Get the damn case and give me back Jeremiah."

Her breath ruffles the curtains. She jolts back, the sudden movement creating more breeze, ruffling the curtain more.

"No, no, no," she whispers. She paces the length of their beat-up futon, clenching and shaking out her hands, clenching, shaking. "Waiting, starving, doing nothing. I'm going to petrify in here. Turn rock solid."

Letting Jeremiah down.

"Come *on*, baby. Walk through the door," she pleads as if he were here. She stares at her pay-as-you-go flip phone, which hasn't made a sound in days. "Tell me what to do."

Jeremiah always knows what to do. Maybe he isn't always right. Maybe he isn't always smart. But he keeps them moving, and movement is something.

A fuck lot better than this prison of an apartment. Where *is* he?

She presses her fingers to her closed eyes and sees him. Tied to a chair, mouth gagged, praying she will figure out that this time it's up to her.

She slams her eyes open, blue and black patches smearing her vision.

Jesus, why hadn't she realized this before. It's up to her, the one who never sees the whole picture. She'll have to figure out their next move.

"No!"

She dashes to the kitchen and heaves her stomach contents into a chipped Fiestaware nesting bowl and crumples soundlessly to the floor.

The evening Jeremiah disappeared, Lena was studying photos of spinning reels at the light box, so she hadn't realized how long he'd been gone until she did. When she finally noticed the time, she put on a bra and a fresh tank top. As the apartment door locked behind her, a smile played on her lips. Jeremiah wasn't selfish very often, so she looked forward to the rare opportunity to tease him for scarfing his dog before bringing hers back.

She pictured his bashful smile, cutting through his black beard. Tall and loose limbed, he had an inky tousle of hair that brushed his long neck. He'd gotten painfully thin lately though. Used to be, he had to stretch his arms above his head before she could see his ribcage. Now his skin cling-wrapped his bones.

Still, walking toward Spike's, Lena found herself appreciating the small pleasures of the day. It was nice to be out of the apartment, even if the evening air was soupy. A few houses had window boxes with petunias and geraniums. Their dewy petals made her want to see more nature. She'd tell Jeremiah she wanted to go for a walk. It would be cooler in the woods, or even at the junky shore.

But he wasn't at Spike's.

She jostled through the line of people waiting for their hot dogs and called, "Hey, Monty, did Jeremiah come in here?"

Monty was a friend of Jeremiah's from way back, high school or middle school maybe. Lena was never sure, but they'd played sports together, soccer and baseball. One day when Monty had been coming over to watch the Celtics game with Jeremiah, on the television they've since pawned, he'd seen the help wanted sign at Spike's and applied. For about five minutes, Jeremiah had been annoyed that Monty beat him to the job. He'd been looking for work for months, ever since he'd been laid off by Tree House. But she'd been glad. Jeremiah was no bun steamer. He wasn't lazy either. He's a talent, made to be outside, digging and pruning, planting and tending. Spinning in the rain.

For a while after he lost his job, he cut lawns, but then he claimed it wasn't worth the price of gas to go begging for lawn work. He told her he spent the days walking the woods along the bay, and for a while, she was too busy to question him. Her catalogue work kept them afloat. Then her work dried up too. Not completely. But enough that she finally had time to look up and wonder where Jeremiah was really spending his time and with whom, and before she'd figured this out, he'd brought home the suitcase.

#

Now, she blinks herself awake and manages to make it to her knees. She crawls to the bathroom where she stands and tries to brush away the taste of bile. After a gum-reddening effort, the taste lingers. She looks at her pale cheeks in the mirror. Her dirty-blond hair is truly dirty and hangs in greasy vines. She hasn't showered since Jeremiah disappeared.

That night, she smelled of hope. The sporting goods shoot was nearly finished, and the suitcase would change their luck. Jeremiah was sure of it, and if she didn't completely trust his vision, she wanted so badly to see him smile again that she convinced herself she did trust him. She hadn't seen him so upbeat in weeks, and she refused to bring him down, to be his grub in the garden, as he would have called her.

"He was supposed to bring me dinner, Monty," she called into Spike's. "Did you see where he went?"

"Nah, Lena, haven't seen him today." Monty shrugged a quick sorry, but the place was busy, and he turned his attention to the hot chili he was ladling onto a chorizo link.

She strolled three blocks to Stop n Go, still taking her time, still thinking of her world as a photograph whose details she saw and understood. She assumed Jeremiah had gone for a newspaper or maybe for smokes. He was trying to quit, but he'd been trying to quit for the three years Lena had known him. Inside the store, Lena grabbed a package of spaghetti, a jar of sauce, and took them to the counter.

"You want scratch cards?" Mr. Hopsik said, smiling. He was always proud when he remembered a regular's usual.

Lena shook her head no. She pulled a few bills from the pocket in her jeans shorts and said, "Have you seen Jeremiah, Mr. Hopsik?"

He said Jeremiah hadn't come in, but he'd seen him getting into a car. When Lena asked what kind of car, he said he couldn't remember. "A nothing kind," he said. "One of those ones that look like all the other ones. He was with a white guy. Shoulders like Toro, a bullock we had when I was a boy, and sort of twitchy-like." Mr. Hopsik jerked his shoulder and head together and nearly slapped his mouth with his limp wrist. "You know that ox-twitch guy?"

Lena shrugged and shook her head. She felt dizzy.

"You okay?" Mr. Hopsik gave her a worried look.

"The heat," she said, forcing a smile, dipping her head toward the fan on the counter. The breeze choked her.

"Oh, this is nothing," he said. "Where I come from . . ."

He went on, but she turned away, letting the guy behind her listen to Mr. Hopsik's story of his native heat.

"Hey," he called as she pushed open the door. "Next time you come in, I'll pick you a winning ticket. You'll see."

Lena waved her thanks.

As she walked home, she cursed that she couldn't call Jeremiah. They'd sold the newer of their pay-as-you-go cellphones, keeping just one so people could contact them for work. They told themselves they were getting used to doing without and were proud their lives were leaner. At night, they lay in bed, each choosing five can't-do-without things. They spent hours revising their lists, using the changes to reveal to each other what they loved and why. Their lean times were only temporary, Jeremiah insisted, and anyway leaner meant simpler, although it rarely felt like that when Lena was washing their clothes in the bathtub.

Walking back toward Spike's, she noticed the gray Mercedes pull up and park. She had half-noticed the car in Stop n Go's parking lot.

Trotting now, she glanced through the car's side window as she passed it, but the windows were tinted what must be an illegal shade of black. When she was steps away from the triple-decker's door, she glanced over her shoulder. Through the windshield, she caught a glimpse of a man with a brush cut and the build of a doorframe. All of a sudden, his torso seized, his arm flew up, and he backhanded his own chin. Ox Twitch.

Panicked, Lena ran to the triple-decker's door. She would return to this moment often, wishing her instinct had been fight not flight. She should have confronted Ox Twitch right then. What if Jeremiah had been in the back seat or the trunk? Instead, she leapt up two flights of stairs and slammed the apartment's door behind her, twisting both deadbolts and shoving the chain lock into its track. She stood frozen, arms wrapped around her ribcage, staring at the door, expecting Ox Twitch and his partner to blast through at any minute.

When no one did, Lena tiptoed to the front window. Dusk blanketed the street, but the SUV glowed under the amber streetlamp that had just switched on. She narrowed her eyes at the vehicle's dark windows and whispered, "Bastards, you better not hurt him. You better not touch one hair."

Lena thought Jeremiah would be back, first in a matter of minutes, then hours. She played the scene of his return over in her mind. He'd come through the door, hand off the case to Ox Twitch or whomever, and get paid or get screwed for his efforts. Either way, she and Jeremiah would laugh—nervously, okay, and with a lot of crying thrown in. But laughing and crying had been their primary coping mechanisms since Jeremiah had been pink-slipped in Chicago.

Hadn't they been doubled over in hysterics when Jeremiah first brought the suitcase back to the apartment after receiving it from snaggle-toothed Dewey from Woonsocket? They treated the whole thing like a lark. Not just Jeremiah, her too. They slid the suitcase under the bed and made love over it fiercely, slapping their bodies together, christening the contents with their sweat for good luck.

The night Jeremiah disappeared, not knowing what else to do, Lena drew the curtains. She cooked enough spaghetti for two. She sat stiffly on the worn microsuede futon and ate, her gaze shifting from door to window to door. She forced herself to get into bed as if it were a regular night and Jeremiah was out with Monty watching a game at a bar.

She lay sleepless for hours, listening, waiting.

Without Jeremiah, the bed felt lumpy, as if the suitcase beneath it had ballooned up and was pressing its corners into her vertebrae. When she did drop off for a while, her dreams were a fevered chaos of hot dogs and scratch cards and unfamiliar alleyways with nonsense names.

In the morning, Lena awoke with a start. She reached out for Jeremiah but only palmed limp sheets.

#

Now choked with thirst and fear and frustration, Lena opens every drawer and cabinet in the kitchen, gathering the few remaining clean dishes and utensils. After putting them on a corner of the counter that was already jammed with smeared dishes, she opens the refrigerator, nearly empty itself, except for a squeeze bottle of brown mustard, a jar of pickle water, three packets of duck sauce, and an open box of baking soda. Lena shakes and squeezes, splashes and spurts the contents of the refrigerator over the last of the clean dishes. She licks every dish, cringing, gagging, and finally coughing as she inhales a lungful of Arm & Hammer.

After licking the potato masher clean—well, not clean but close enough—she closes her eyes and whispers, "Hang on, Jeremiah."

Then she showers, thrusting her head past the shower curtain to throw up again into the toilet. As she dresses, she runs through both her own and Jeremiah's five-things-you-can't-do-without lists. She packs hers fast. Then she does her best to collect Jeremiah's list items, but she can't find the little trowel charm she'd given him for his last birthday. It's the only item of jewelry he owns, and he doesn't wear it often, so it's usually on their dresser top, ready to be pawned next. Was he wearing it the night he disappeared?

She can't see why he would have been, so she kneels and searches the matted carpeting near the bedside table. Patting beneath the bed, her fingers brush the hard shell of the suitcase, and she retracts her hand as if burned.

After a moment, she reaches under the bed again, this time deliberately feeling for the suitcase's handle. She wraps her fingers around it and slides the suitcase out. With it comes a shoebox-size steel lockbox she's never seen before.

She lifts the suitcase onto the bed and places the steel box beside it, amazed that any container can shoot anxiety through her more than that suitcase does.

Biting on both thumbnails at the same time, she considers not opening either the suitcase or the box. Leave them both behind, and maybe she'll shake off those people, whoever they are. The answer seems obvious until it occurs to her that she'd be leaving Jeremiah behind too. She'll have nothing to bargain with if bargaining becomes necessary.

What would Jeremiah do?

Slow down, she hears him say. Eyes closed, she feels herself swaying. Instinctively she reaches out for Jeremiah's arm to steady herself, but her hand meets the wooden back of the chair.

Open it, he whispers.

Letting go of the chair, she stares at the box, then clicks the latch. Inside she finds a small gun.

She can see this is a gun meant for purses or pockets. Her experience with guns is limited but not nonexistent. In the rural Midwest where she grew up, teaching kids to shoot is considered on par with teaching kids to swim; if you don't have a swimming pool in your backyard, some other family does. Lena's mother had taught her how to handle a gun when she was eight years old.

So the gun's potential in and of itself isn't so disturbing to her. It's occurred to her before to suggest to Jeremiah that they get one, but it seemed frivolous when they didn't have enough money for an air conditioner or rent for the apartment to put it in. Besides, he'd always expressed disdain for gun owners, assuming they're either gangsters or the kind of people who believe in conspiracy theories, who spend weekends bivouacking with backwoods buddies. We're not gangsters, she assumed he'd say.

But Jeremiah had gone out and bought one, presumably. Or had someone given it to him? Either way, he snuck the gun into the apartment, never bothering to tell her she was sleeping on top of one, giving them no opportunity to disarm its existence with lame cracks about wanting to create sparks in the bedroom or adding a bang to their bucking.

Jeremiah had been too afraid to joke.

Simultaneously, she takes a step back and reaches out for the gun. Her reach wins out. Her hand naturally curls around the grip. She checks to see if it's loaded. It is.

"Jesus, Jeremiah," she whispers. "You let me sleep over a loaded gun. I'm fucking pregnant!"

Forgetting herself, she sweeps her arms wide as she would if he were standing before her. The gun slips from her hand and flies across the room. She gasps, but it falls to the carpet without going off.

She glares at it, then sighs and picks it up.

She returns to the box, searching for additional bullets. Instead, she finds a note. She hesitates only a moment before unfolding it and reading. Written in black magic marker, in Jeremiah's crooked script, the message is different from the notes they usually write to each other—*gone to pick up toilet paper* or *your brother called*. This one is oddly formal, with both a greeting and a signature.

Dear Lena, Use it if you have to. I'm sorry, babe. Yours forever, Jer.

She drops the note onto the mattress and backs away from it.

Only later, as she's zipping her duffle closed does she realize she still holds the gun. She places it and the note in the box, closes it, and shoves the loaded box into the bottom of her bag.

She waits an hour, until darkness solidifies. She uses the time to finalize the selections for the photo shoot, slipping the negatives and proofs into a FedEx envelope. She sends an email to Warren, her contact at Vista Media, telling him the negatives and proofs are on their way and asking him to direct deposit her check into her bank account as soon as possible.

She spends the rest of the time looking through the break in the curtains, but not at the street. She looks out over the sad field and the woods beyond, her gaze trained on the falling sun. As the tree tips pierce the sun's orange yolk, a sense of her aloneness saturates her. She can't remember a time she's been so completely alone.

Jeremiah is gone. Of course he is.

I'm sorry, babe.

Sorry for what, she'd like to scream. For disappearing? For the suitcase? For the last two excruciating days of what-the-fuck? Was he sorry for what's to come? Or was he sorry for everything they'd been and done?

She listens and looks, and when no answer comes, she realizes she's begun using the past tense for Jeremiah. She circles her belly with her palm and says soothingly to her stomach, "It will be fine." It's her responsibility to envision a future.

She turns the radio on before she slides the balcony's door shut behind her. Despite everything, the absurdity of actually tiptoeing to the Ranger makes her smile. Jeremiah will laugh when she tells him this. *Will. Would.* Her smile turns to a hard line.

She tosses the duffle onto the truck's passenger seat. With a shove, she stashes the suitcase into the extended cab space behind the driver's seat and covers it with one of the empty burlap sacks Jeremiah uses—used to use—to protect a sapling's roots. She climbs in, turns the ignition key slowly, and shifts to neutral, headlights off. With nearly unbearable slowness, gravity does its work, pulling the truck not back toward the street but forward, toward the weedy turf of the open lot and the tree line. With momentum on her side, she starts the engine and guns it. When the tires fishtail on the slick grass, she grips the steering wheel tighter to help her keep her nerve. In the darkness, she aims for the path in the woods, hoping her mind's eye is true and the path will be wide enough for the truck to bullet through and away.

Tollways

Crosshairs

Just when you make a resolution to become truly happy, that rat bastard Misery throws off his coat, drips slush on your hardwoods, and settles in for the dark, cold night of your life.

Glaring at a hundred angled reflections of herself in the Brides of Paradise mirrors, Genevieve resigns herself to marrying Oscar and having the child they so carelessly created.

"Happiness be damned."

Snarling, she shoves a finger between the bodice stays and her engorged breasts. Fabric won't give a millimeter.

"For eff's sake," she mutters.

When she awoke that snowy morning with her head aching, why hadn't she whipped up a Bloody Mary cure instead of rolling over and reaching for Oscar? She tugs at the girder of chiffon.

"Hair of the dog, Genevieve," she whispers so the wolfish saleswoman won't hear her remorse. "*Not* doggie style. Hair. Of. The. Dog."

But no amount of drinker's remorse can help her now. She rakes her fingernails over the champagne-pink netting encasing her belly.

Things had been going so well.

Damn if she hadn't just gotten promoted. Okay, maybe not to a job she liked. But she didn't like any job, didn't like to work at all. Who in their right mind did?

"Why they call it *work*," her father used to say to her irritation.

When discussing who would fill the position of air charters coordinator now that Gloria Sylvester was finally leaving the travel incentive company (to make a go of the pottery-painting shop she'd droned on about every damn day for the past five years), Genevieve's supervisors hadn't exactly been enthusiastic. Lawrence, head of charter air and bus sales, expressed concern Genevieve and Gloria shared the same first initial. "Only way I know who to yell at for my clients' screwed-up charters is by the initials on each order. *G-G-G-Genevieve* will blame it all on *G-G-G-Gloria*. *S-S-S-Susan* is a clearer choice."

"For Christ's sake, Lawrence, look at the second letter," said Wendy, promotions director. "What we really need is someone detail-oriented."

"In that race, Genevieve snaps the tape before Susan's off the starting block," said Dianne, Genevieve's current supervisor. "Picky to a fault, that's Genevieve. To a tee." Critical of everyone. And everything, Dianne added to herself. Dianne could do with a little less picky criticism in her department. A little less whining too. Genevieve is a great whiner. Already, Dianne had been eyeing a mute little chipmunk in accounting to replace Genevieve.

Lawrence clinched it for Genevieve by pointing out the need for someone easily motivated by the free perks the bus companies and airlines gave them, things like cheap nylon bags with swirling logos and paperweights in the shapes of miniature airplanes with cut crystal wings. "The position involves long hours with no overtime pay," Lawrence said. "Baubles are the only real compensation."

"Genevieve loves that shit!" Dianne chirped. "Her desk is piled with tchotchke crap."

And so, Genevieve it was.

When Genevieve was told of her promotion, three good things had already happened to her. First, she caught the express train into the Loop and found a seat that didn't have the remains of vomit or fast food on it. And it hadn't cost her a minute's sleep either. The express train had been fifteen minutes late. Sure, other people were pissing and moaning at the tardy train. They were going to be late for work, a few may even be fired, but for once Genevieve was ahead of schedule. "Suckers," she hissed quietly, settling into her relatively unsullied seat.

Second, she had time to stop at the place with the really *good* coffee, The Knockout Café. The barista mistakenly poured Genevieve the heavyweight size instead of the bantamweight one she had ordered. Genevieve didn't offer to pay the difference. It wasn't her fault the woman got it wrong. What's more, Genevieve saved on a tip since she wasn't about to reward someone who got her order wrong.

Finally, when she got to work, someone else had cured the ailing client file that sickened her so badly yesterday that she'd finally given it up for terminally ill and gone to happy hour at The Stagger Inn to clear her head. And she wasn't even hung over this morning.

"Good days like this can make you believe happiness is more than slurry bar talk," she affirmed to her beige cube walls.

A moment later, Dianne told Genevieve about the promotion. Dianne looked so happy Genevieve instantly altered the impression she'd had that Dianne thought she was surly and an idiot besides. Dianne must have tilted at the windmill of management for her. Genevieve never expected such a show of loyalty and support from Dianne, never expected such success for herself. Flushed, she embraced Dianne.

"You won't regret it."

"I know," said Dianne.

Genevieve felt caught in the crosshairs of happiness.

"Let the joy bullet brain me," she trilled, packing up her desk for the move from her beige cube to her own private office. Okay, the office was also beige, dinky, and without windows, but it had three shelves. She would keep one shelf exclusively for the snow globes, airplane paperweights, and mounted golf balls that had been the forecasters of her inevitable success. And she would collect more of these free gems in her new position.

She lugged the shockingly heavy canvas bag with *Say 'Aloha!' to Hawaii!* scrawled across the front of it from her scuffed cube desk to her scarred office desk.

"Happiness is gunning for me," she called to all the beige walls in the world. "Shoot me now."

Then she threw up.

Into her bag of promotional treasures and onto the spritely glass hands of the Peter Pan Bus Company pencil holder.

\#

That had been less than a week ago. Now she's spending her Saturday stuck in a bridal shop planning her funeral. She chides herself for being so dramatic. Marrying Oscar and having his baby isn't death. Not exactly. More like sinking into muddy quicksand. She peels off the chiffon, thinking his drab love will so mire her in sludge she won't be able to move.

At least he loves her. He'd nosed around the marriage question before he found the pregnancy test stick in the bathroom wastebasket.

Good lord, she realizes with alarm, she's marrying a man who roots around in other people's bathroom wastebaskets. She nearly throws up again but holds herself back. She doesn't want to have to buy this chiffon monstrosity. She doesn't want to waste good money on anything in this ice-cream cake of a store.

"Should have taken that test stick straight outside," she mutters into the raspberry taffeta the clerk hands her through the curtain as her next try-on.

Oscar's so delighted there's no giving him the slip now. He'll track her scent the rest of her life if she doesn't marry him. He'll sniff her out at work, at the gym, booby-trap her on the way to the women's health center. He'll ruin her life and take himself down with her.

Better to surrender, which she unintentionally did when he showed up with a ring.

He'd caught her in a weakened condition. She'd been sick all day, her body violently rejecting the twist of fate that had drowned her mewling kitten of happiness. Oscar had come bearing a bottle of plain seltzer.

She saw it and cried, "That's just what I want. How did you know?"

Oscar believed she was referring to the diamond ring he had tied with a silk ribbon to the neck of the soda bottle. Elated, he unrung the neck and shoved the gold band with a sizeable diamond over her knuckle, kissing the gathered skin he ripped along the way.

"Do you like it? Really?"

With her gaze trained on the seltzer bubbling inside the green-tinted glass, she said, "I'm so thirsty for it."

Oscar popped the bottle's cap. She loosened her throat and guzzled, rivulets drooling over her cheeks and chin.

Now when she thinks of that moment, she remembers a nature show she'd seen where a lion cut off a weak wildebeest from the herd, wrangling it down, dragging it away to devour in its den. Oscar has a den with wall-to-wall oak bookshelves and dusty, unread books and sneaky pocket doors that only appear once they're closing you in.

As Genevieve struggles into the raspberry dress, the ring's diamond catches and rips the taffeta bustle.

"Ring's got teeth," she laments, examining the tear. "I can't possibly buy something so ridiculous for a shotgun wedding."

She removes the dress and drops it in a confused heap that she hopes hides the rip. She hurries into her jeans and sweater and out of the shop.

Shotgun wedding. She hasn't been able to get the phrase out of her mind since Oscar ringed her. On her way to her car, when she passes a sporting goods store with hunting gear in the window, she stops.

The green camouflage is so much prettier than anything in the wedding store. Two mannequins are positioned as if pulling bows. Another has a knife strapped to his hand, kneeling over a taxadermied deer. Forced onto its back, its legs sprung in the air, the animal fights against the moment of death. She can't decide if she feels admiration or disgust for the hunter, compassion or bloodlust for the deer.

Hunter or hunted? Which is she?

Her uncertainty propels her inside the store where she feels more at ease than in the wedding dress store. Mud-colored clothing, tents with dead-leaf designs, strange contraptions made for perching in trees for hours on end, they're all full of intent. Bows, arrows, shotguns, knives. They would look terrific on her shelf at work next to the globes and hula dancers that she'd been able to salvage from her vomit.

She strolls the aisles, fingering leg-and-body traps, animal-restraint poles, game calls, and lure scents. Everything is designed to make death easier.

Is life anything more than one long hunting season, she wonders.

In the clothing section, she steps into thigh-high waders and elbows herself into a grass-colored flak jacket. The jacket drowns her, but in a few months, when she's the hippopotamus she's sure to be on the day of the wedding, it might fit just right.

She finds a mirror. Impressed with the figure she cuts, she hunkers into positions one might assume while awaiting prey. She fake shoots, hitting every pretend target dead center.

Then she stops shooting and splays on the ground, her legs in the same position as the deer in the window. The position she'll assume in childbirth?

Lying on the hard tile, she returns other customers' curious looks with an imitation of the deer's expression.

Hunter or prey?

She'd been sure Oscar was out to trap her and kill her happiness. But isn't marriage a trap for two?

"At each other's mercy for life," she whispers.

She flips onto her wader-covered knees.

Psheeewww.

She can kill his happiness just as he can kill hers.

In line to purchase the jacket for her wedding day, she decides on a woodsy location, a jerky charcuterie spread for the reception. Beside her, ruddy-faced men grip rain ponchos and tree stools designed to make the wait for death more comfortable in inclement weather. When things are miserable, you cling to comfort. But after a time, these items will become unbearable. The poncho will droop from rain and perspiration; the tree stool will scream against hemorrhoids. Is there no comfort anywhere? In the hunt, is misery itself the comfort?

She wears the jacket out of the store and into a wall of bitter-cold air. She wonders what Oscar has done all day. Lifting her chin to the sky, she exposes her jugular to the wind. She buttons the jacket's fur-lined collar tighter, but it still hangs loosely about the tender skin of her slim neck.

She strides to her car, her nostrils flared, her gaze scoping.

Some Damage

The element of surprise was crucial for the hunt. An expert in the dark, Swift was trained to wait. Lying next to her wife, Brin, in the bed they shared, she counted Brin's breaths. She would wait.

The only woman in her gun club to earn the status of night-sharpshooter, Swift hunted deer when they least expected her. Used to be, Brin stripped skin and bone from the animals Swift killed. One day though, rather than smiling approvingly at Swift when she stood in the doorway holding up the day's kill, Brin squashed her face in disgust.

"You ever think about how graceful deer are, Swift?" she said, her hand stuck to her side, refusing to caress the carcass's pelt as she often did.

"Ballerinas of the woods, huh?"

"Well, now that you say it, yes, something like that."

"Nah. Ballerinas ain't got an ounce of fat." She shook the carcass that was straining her shoulder. "This one's a marbled beauty."

"You're disgusting," she said, gesturing for Swift to take the animal back outside to the butchering shed.

Swift retreated, but Brin's comments were disturbing. In the shower, washing blood and dirt from her body, Swift tried to swipe away the bad taste Brin's expression had left.

Swift got enough of that crap from townies, who were all the time saying the hunters had no feeling for animals. Accused her of lacking compassion. Crissakes, who spent more time in the very woods those deer lived in, thinking on their movements, their behaviors, their preferences? The townies who bought cows and chickens all packaged neat from supermarkets? No, goddamn it. Swift slept on the same wet leaves the does did with their fawns. She studied their lives, got to know which animals had young, which were lame, which smart, which mean. Least she had the respect to receive the animals' stunned expressions. She gave the animals enough credit to believe their looks the moment before she pulled the trigger meant they believed they were seeing their god.

By the time she dried off and slathered herself with some of Brin's vanilla-scented lotion, she'd managed to laugh off the encounter. Brin was no townie. They'd been living in the way out of Privy for a decade now. And Brin was a hearty eater. Swift loved this about her, that she slapped and smacked her lips. Brin let grease smear her fingers. She wiped but didn't wash those hands right after a meal, so Swift could smell her satisfaction on her skin when Brin bent to kiss Swift with lips made supple by fat. Lordy sakes, how she loved Brin then. How she loved her always. Swift's emotions filled her up and bowled her over.

But that night at supper, Brin ate the venison stew she'd cooked, but with less gusto than usual, and she went to bed early, not kissing Swift goodnight.

#

In the days that followed, Brin often gave Swift that squashed look of disgust. Plenty of times, it had nothing to do with hunting. Swift didn't say anything. She believed her mother's adage, least said, soonest mended. She told herself it was nothing, her imagination. Brin was still her Brin.

After a week of Brin bulleting lip curls at her, Swift had to acknowledge her wife was changing. Swift hated change. Even seasonal shifts disturbed her equilibrium. It had never seemed right that the sun should set at four in the afternoon in winter, at nine in summer. Of course, she understood the earth's axis and rotation, but she didn't approve of them or their shiftiness. And she did not like this change in Brin one bit. Swift missed her. Brin's rebuffs of affection and food left Swift feeling wounded.

It used to be that on freezing winter nights, with ice caking the windows of their small lakeside shack, they lay in bed, and Brin circled the scar on Swift's hip with her fingertip. With her tongue she licked and cooed a soft prayer, "Tell me again."

"The lead that shattered me is like my love for you," Swift repeated each time. "I carry it with me everywhere." She didn't tell Brin that the scar sometimes burned when her emotions toward Brin were strongest. When Brin wasn't there, Swift's fingers instinctively circled the scar's ridges and striations.

Before Brin's change, Swift hugged Brin's body in bed. Brin always seemed cold, as if there weren't enough blood to reach her fingertips and toes. Swift recited the details of the bullet she carried in her muscle as if it were a love poem. "My love for you is a Swift A-frame, 25-caliber, 100-grain, bonded semi-spitzer."

"Is it a good one?"

"Not the biggest," Swift admitted, her fleshy paw resting on the delicate bones of Brin's back. "Enough to do some damage."

"And it's where you got your nickname?" Brin said, her face shadowed in the half-light of the moon, her eyes as bright as those on the deer Swift shot. At these moments, Brin had made Swift feel, not godlike—no, Swift wouldn't go that far—but that she was substantial. Flesh and blood.

But no longer. Brin's gaze now looked past Swift. At what, Swift wanted to know. For weeks, Brin remained distant, and Swift remained puzzled.

One day, when Brin was out, Swift rifled through the galley kitchen in the corner of the shack, looking for tin cans to use for target practice. She couldn't find a single can, not of beans or corn or peas. Where the cans usually lived, she found a ceramic mixing bowl with hearts etched into the side. She'd never seen the bowl before.

It looked amateurish. A child's camp project. But she hardly gave it a thought. Instead, she drew a buck head on a paper grocery bag, pinned it to a tree, and shot, shot, shot. Bang. Hitting a target dead center usually gave Swift grave satisfaction. But by the time she'd spent a box of bullets, she felt nothing. My heart is a hollow chamber, she thought.

At dinner that evening, Swift forgot to ask Brin about the heart bowl, but she asked why they had no canned goods in the cabinet. "Bad snowstorm, we'll be stuck."

Brin rolled her eyes.

Swift's scar pinched suddenly. How could Brin dismiss their reality so easily? Swift kept her temper though. "Brin, baby, don't you remember back—what, four, five years ago?—when the snow piled so high, it took a week to chip our way out the transom?"

Brin shrugged. "I like fresh veg now. Canned's gross."

Swift was surprised at how hurt she felt. Rejection of the canned goods felt like one more rejection of her. She managed to respond with a grunt she hoped was neutral. But her scar itched with pain.

Of course, now that Brin had mentioned it, Swift realized that lately two, three times a week, Brin had been driving the fifty miles into town to the nearest supermarket. When they had provisions, she only went every other week. Swift chewed an undercooked green bean, her scar burning now, all joy in their meal gone.

Puzzled, Swift told her hunting pal, Gordo, about it one evening when they were cleaning guns and drinking whiskey at the gun club.

"Not too swift, are you, Swift?" Gordo said. "No one needs to buy onions every day."

Swift cocked her head in confusion.

"Bang-bang," Gordo added, not making a gun with her hand but rubbing her crotch.

"Oh." Swift said. She stared into the barrel of her gun to avoid looking Gordo in the eye.

Now, lying in the dark, Swift listened to her wife's breath. When it took on the rhythm that signaled Brin's deepest sleep, Swift crawled out of bed and slid into the headlight slippers Brin had given her for her last birthday. She pulled the mixing bowl from the cabinet, pulled off one slipper, and shined the toe light on the backside of the bowl.

In the circle of light she read the stamp: Pat's Pottery.

Swift's hand shook. She wanted to slam it, smash it, toss it high, aim her rifle, and chug-chug-chug the damn thing to nothing. But Swift forced her training to kick in. Swift was a waiter. She would wait.

She turned off her footlight. In the dark, Swift made her way back to the bed where her wife slept soundly. Lids blinking blurred tears in the dark, she waited. She placed the bowl on the kitchen counter without a chip.

The next morning Swift rousted herself early. She didn't glance at the bowl on the counter. Instead, she cleaned her guns at the kitchen table.

When Brin saw the bowl on the counter, she hesitated, stutter-stepped, then grabbed it and used it to mix pancake batter. The lemon poppy-seed pancakes felt like sand in Swift's mouth, but she ate them, telling herself that today flapjacks were camouflage.

She watched Brin fuss about in the bedroom, scooping shirts, socks, anything within reach into a sack. Then with the sack in her hands and her faux fur coat buttoned and belted, Brin announced, "I'm going into town to do the laundry and some shopping."

Swift nodded. She waited a moment after the door slammed before grabbing her Ruger 9mm. She hopped into her truck. Keeping at least six car lengths between them, Swift followed Brin. At first she was heartened. Brin stopped at the laundromat, just as she said she would. Maybe Gordo had been wrong. Gordenia was none too swift herself. Swift waited, hoping for redemption. From across the street, she scoped Brin until she left the laundromat, the near-empty sack in one hand, Swift's headlamp slippers in the other.

On foot, Swift trailed Brin by half a block. Brin's fur coat swayed with each prancing step, and the beauty of the movement nearly broke Swift's heart. If not for her training, she would have felt a fool ducking into doorways when she feared being spotted, but hunting required shiftiness. She knew that.

Swift was sure she felt the bullet in her hip shift when Brin pulled open the door to Pat's Pottery. Through the glass, Swift watched Brin kiss a thin-waisted human in a ponytail. Pat? Probably.

Swift backed away from the window, the glare of the morning sun blinding her. In the empty light, Swift pictured Brin, her bare legs wrapped around that skinny waist, Swift's own headlamp slippers dangling from Brin's feet, the lights throwing patterns across Pat's pots, which smelled of earth, not flesh.

Swift yearned to run, but that kiss had nailed Swift to the spot like the deer she stunned. She knew now those deer had never seen Swift as any kind of god. They despised Swift as she now despised Brin. Helpless and heart sore and staggered by all they were about to lose, those deer wanted to kill Swift for hate and not sport or even food.

"Oh, God!" Brin yelled so loudly the words shot through Pat's walls. "Oh, my sweet, sweet God."

Swift's ears pricked up even as her legs buckled. The smack of the concrete against her kneecap brought her back to herself. She touched her bullet scar. Then she folded her fist around the Ruger and leapt to her feet. Pain loaded her adrenaline, and she darted for the store, gun at her hip.

Through the front window, she saw them, Brin's eyes, wide and stunned and when they when they locked on Swift's, sad.

No, they said. *No.*

Those eyes dropped Swift like that bullet that had felled her all those years ago. She lowered the gun and turned away, heading home alone.

A Fair

Our final act. We agreed. One last night.

When the carnival comes to town, you have to go.

Squealing children. Cheap games. Tinny music. The lights, a thousand constellations. Grotesque and glorious, side by side. Like us.

Let's make it memorable. Memory is all we'll have.

Dizzy. Dancing. The way it looks in a film. The way we'd felt all along.

Hidden in the crowds, we strolled as if the entire world had cameras aimed at us.

Let's get high.

I said? Or you said?

Without saying so, or maybe we did say, you or I, as we slid thigh to thigh, ribcage to ribcage, curling into our ending like closing parentheses, we said, offhandedly, or didn't say, but certainly we assumed (who doesn't? who gets on the Ferris wheel without assuming?): the carnival people perform regular maintenance on the rides.

Don't they?

Did we mean everything we said, or did we play to an audience of two?

Keep belts, ponytails, scarves, and neckties secured. Hands inside at all times. The skeletal boy instructed in teenage monotone. He lowered the bar so we wouldn't fall out. Caramel and weed and boredom rose from his skin.

Who wears a necktie on a Ferris wheel? You asked the boy. Or I asked?
Dunno. He chomped his gum and shrugged on.

Of course, we both knew someone who would wear a tie. And another someone who wouldn't dare ride at all. Ghosts beside us in the seats.

A three-minute ride is a thrill.

After all, we loved them. Our ghosts. Just. A last whirl. A twirl to last a lifetime.

See the Serpent Man Shed Skin! Watch the Acrobat Hair Hanger! Test Your Skill Piloting the Drone! Shoot Ducks in a Barrel! Win a Prize!

On the top of the world, the neon lights coiled into a thousand fractals.

Arms entwined, we trilled the old Carpenters song, insisting it was insipid, but we knew all the words. We changed them to suit us. *Up here unshaven . . . You're my fixation . . . Upward rotation . . .* Our laughter shivered the seat. We squealed, gleeful at the last.

We'd made it. Kept our secret to the end.

Colorful lights below. Stars above. We shone.

When you hug an apparition, do your arms ache?

I love your eyebrows and fingers.
The curve of your foot's arch.
Your hair falling past your shoulder blades where angel wings attach
to fly you to heaven.

Arial hair-hanging is an ancient and exotic act.

We flew and fell. Round and round.

A Ferris wheel has only so many twirls before the gears break. Or the bolts securing the seats loosen. Or brace legs snap. Hub and spindle detach. Steel cables shred.

Isn't failure inevitable? Isn't breakage built in?

No sudden movements! No rocking! The boy's voice broke with boredom.

It was too dark to see vast landscapes. The cityscape though. *Just look!* We traced the paths to our houses, searching for connections. Your open windows stared wide-eyed. Mine were closed, shaded lenses.

If they could see us now. Here. Together. Oh God, just imagine! We didn't like to. Not too much. But tonight. At the last. *Imagine!* We needed them. A thrill.

Aren't forever secrets an intimacy too?

Suddenly, our descent was a jiggery plummet.

Ah!

We hit bottom, and chugged up, up up!

Thrilling.

Everyone loves a little danger.

Isn't this, at least a bit, why we loved each other?

If we're honest.

We were at eleven o'clock when the wheel froze.

Near-apex.

We laughed. Nervously.

Do actors change their performances when they know the curtain is closing for good?

Surely the fire trucks and ambulances are just precautions. You said, or maybe it was me. We scooched closer.

Should we have slid as far apart as the seat allowed? Sought balance?

When the thrill settles, nerves unhinge.

Two hours.

Did we love each other?

Stuck and swaying.

Boredom simmers.

Until. All those phones winking.

It's too dark for them to see us, right?

You said.

Too far?

We coiled and swayed and hid our faces.

Our final act.

After all, we didn't want to hurt them. Our ghosts.

A drone buzzed.

Does that fucking thing have a camera?

When the thrill rises, horror descends.

We didn't want to be hurt either.

If you know it's the last time, does it mean more?

Stay calm, riders! We're nearly there. A firefighter bull-horned.

The drone buzzed.

Our final act.

Buzzzzzzzzzz.

Who doesn't swat at a wasp when it torments?

In a frenzy. You swished.

Gonna. Fucking. Kill. It!

The big wheel shimmied.

Aren't carnivals all about gluttony?

Funnel cakes. Cotton candy. Ice cream all day long.

If we were honest.

Our seat swayed. But the bolts held.

I love the way your hair falls.

The drone zipped away.

You couldn't stop.

Leaning over the safety bar to make one last grab.

Your whirling arms.

I couldn't.

Awakening gears.

Screech. And turn.

The crowd cheered.

I yelped.

A hundred phone cameras flashed like the northern lights.

A thousand.

A million.

Marvel at the Acrobat Hair Hanger!

Caught.

I'm scalped!

You. Hanging by a handful of strands.

It takes three minutes for a hydraulic-piston rod to raise a fire truck's aerial ladder.

A three-second fall is a horror.

A thrill.

Our finale. We agreed.

Hanging by a strand.

Did we mean anything?

If we're honest, weren't we all?

Hanging.

All.

Then.

. . .

164

The photos were spectacular.

A thousand brilliant lights.

Fast
Lane

Thresholds

"I'm not going to the park," Vivian said, one bare foot inside the house, the other on the foyer's rough stone. Holding the screen door open, she rocked gently, foot to foot, inside and out. She admired her toenails, a different color for each toe. The rainbow made her think of jelly beans or crayons. Embarrassed, she discarded these associations for an array of lipsticks she and Shannon had seen at the drugstore when they stopped on their way home from school. Cool and sleek, that's what her toes were.

"You are going," replied her mother, shoving diapers and a bottle of apple juice into the back of the stroller. The baby whined at being jostled, and Vivian's mom had to resist the urge to pinch those tiny lips between her fingers. It would be satisfying to see them squished together, soundless, struggling, but quiet. What she wouldn't give for five goddamn seconds of quiet.

"No," Vivian whined. She grabbed onto the handle of the screen door but didn't open it further. The crease between her mother's eyebrows meant her mother was on edge again. Her mother was always on edge since Charlie. Did Vivian dare push her? There would be a scene. Oh, God! Anyone could pass while her mother yelled. But her mother was so dull and heavy. Shannon was color and light, music and moving her body like birds' wings. She loved to hear Shannon's breath.

"March!" her mother said, already pushing the stroller down the path to the sidewalk. She didn't glance back, afraid her girl would see doubt in her eyes. Everything threatened to spin off like the tops she spun for Charlie. How much longer could she keep it under control?

Shannon's favorite song played softly from the headphones draped around Vivian's neck. Her mother's scarred mules scraped the path, the tendons at her ankles taut white. When her mother turned onto the sidewalk, Vivian saw a brown smear smudging her mother's calf. Ugh! Charlie's poo! *Shit*, she corrected herself. Charlie's shit! Oh, God, they'd pass Shannon's house!

Still barefoot, she pushed the screen, leapt onto the porch, and ran down the steps. She had to get her mother to come back. Her mother's humiliation was hers too. As Vivian ran, a shard from a smashed Colt 45 bottle cut into her arch; she limp-hopped, then hopped-hopped her pain, finally tumbling onto the cement, her elbow and the heel of her hand scraped raw.

"No!" she called.

Still walking, her mother exhaled. It would be okay. It would be okay. It would. As long as she did not turn around. The girl had to come on her own. Come back to them. *And if she didn't?* "No," she spit, fisting the stroller's handles. *She had to. She would.*

"No, Mom!" Vivian called as her mother turned the corner, out of sight, toward Shannon's. Blood drooled from Vivian's foot.

"Mommy, please," she whispered.

Her mother walked steadily on but slowed her steps.

Come on, Viv. Come back to us.

Charlie screeched, and she stumbled.

Anchor

Back then, when I perched in my tree, the maple leaves could conceal my whole hand. The breeze off Lake Milfoil shivered my hair. I fit perfectly between trunk and branch. I could have relaxed there if my anticipation hadn't kept my every muscle tensed. High above the bike path, cyclists whooshed beneath me. Parents pushed strollers with screaming or sleeping children. Dogs and their walkers scissored or strolled, the noses of the former lifting curiously at my tree.

I hardly noticed those things, so busy was I, watching for Eliot, who passed this way each morning on his way home from swimming practice. Like a sailor's widow, I scanned the horizon, my eyes squinting on the point where he would exit the soybean fields and enter the park. His biking was unique, and I could pick him out instantly, the bounce of his black curls, the list of his shoulders as he leaned into his stride. He rode with a surprising gawkiness for a boy as graceful as he was in the pool where his attack on the water and stopwatch were as smooth as any bird hunting insects in flight. Although easily distracted, he was a confident cyclist, popping wheelies with ease.

Although I perched for a month of mornings, he only spotted me once. That day, rain drooped the maple's leaves, so my red sneakers must have been visible. Or perhaps I shifted just as Eliot glanced up, and the shimmy of the branch caught his eye. Whatever the reason, he looked up. Our gazes met, and my intake of breath was so sharp my throat choked. His smile was instant. He knew me. And he smiled!

As he pedaled closer, he leaned back onto his saddle in what I knew was his preparation for riding no-hands. In a flash I imagined him reaching for me, and me leaping from my branch and into his extended arms. I moved from crouch to squat, ready to fly to him just like those birds.

To this day, he denies reaching up. Not that we talk of that day. He can't stand to remember how free he used to be. I can't stand to see the accusation in his eyes at having been the one who caused him to take his attention from the path before him. He missed the stone in the path, and his tire caught.

On another day, the one before or after, both of which were bone dry, he might have righted himself. Or if he'd kept his grip on his handlebars, he might have swerved and straightened.

But rain and what we later determined to be bike oil had slicked the blacktop. Eliot slid and slammed into my tree, shaking me from my perch. I landed on him, neither elegantly nor joyfully but crushingly.

He would not marry me. I asked him many times over the next years, point-blank, "Be my husband. Let me take care of you."

"It isn't your fault." His face seemed to have withered with his legs. The smile that used to light his eyes, the one he shined on me when he saw me above him, withered too. I only ever saw his teeth when he ate the chocolate cakes I baked for him, the only sweetness he would accept from me. Even then, his lips seemed to snarl at my efforts as he bit.

"I love you," I said.

"I won't burden anyone."

"Love is no burden."

Each time, he shook his black curls. "No." He twirled his wheelchair away from me with an elegance he'd never managed on his bike. "Please, just leave me alone."

I did. I would do anything for him.

One year after he sent me away, he married Josie. I saw them once in Olga's buying groceries. In the fresh vegetable section, he and Josie tossed grapes into each other's mouths. His smile was back. And his laugh. He'd shaved off his black curls. I felt an overwhelming urge to kiss his bony skull. He seemed to have gotten used to his leglessness. He wheelied his chair as he'd done with his bicycle.

With his front wheels in the air, he spotted me by the broccoli. His chair dropped with a slam, grapes spilling to the floor.

To my shame, I fled.

Josie spit after me, "Leave us alone, you crazy loon! You've done a lifetime's damage already!"

Did I imagine Eliot yelling after me, "I do not forgive you"?

#

The cyclists are first. I feel a whoosh each time a racer cuts through the air below me. I cling to the maple's branches, arm over arm, leg over leg. It's harder to see this way, but I can take no chance of falling. I have taken no chances. Love is nothing in the face of shame.

Leaves slap my cheeks. I blow them away, too frightened to let go of my limbs to brush them aside. Climbing up, my body cried out that it is no longer a child's. The scrape of age bleeds my shin. I wind the rope tighter around me. I retie the knot I have spent months practicing, progressing from yarn to laundry line to this double-braid rappelling rope that binds me to this tree.

Time lags after the last cyclist passes. Awaiting my drop, my limbs ache. But Eliot, his shrunken legs, his bald head, his smile for Josie. I tighten my hold, keep my stance.

When the pack of wheelchair racers emerges from the soybean fields, Eliot leads, but only just. He's wheel to wheel with another racer. My toes tense inside my old red sneakers. All his youthful gawkiness is gone. He swims through air, stroke, stroke, determination as good as joy. He pulls ahead, widens the gap. His sweat glistens, so when he passes below me, the whoosh that rises is sweet and musky, and I inhale and hold the breath. Love. Forgiveness. I hold tight to the branches and let him go.

When Shopping for Colonoscopy Underwear

The last thing you want is to run into your ex-lover, who is many things but not your same sex and not trans and absolutely not fluid about anything, least of all sexuality, and is therefore shopping for lingerie for some other new cis lover.

Fingering silk?

Those fingers . . . remember?

What should you do?

Jump into the aisle and shout, "You never bought *me* intimates! Smart-wool climbing socks don't count"?

Or grab a peach teddy and brush it over your lover's face as you walk away without a word?

Tell the salesperson to call security because there's a known pedophile, who looks suspicious and might be buying an extra-extra-small powder-pink baby doll for nefarious intentions?

Knock over a rack, domino the next three, hoping the last one punctures your lover's brain?

Drop to your knees before those familiar Doc Martens, palms pressed together, and whisper, "I'll pray for your soul, but it probably won't help"?

Drop to your knees before those familiar Doc Martens, cradle your lover's chunky calves, and plead, "Please drive me home from my colonoscopy; I'll be weak with hunger"?

Drop to your knees before those familiar Doc Martens, lead with one shoulder, rugby tackle your lover, and spit, "You broke my heart; I break your spine"?

Watch as your lover selects the same poly-cotton bra-and-panty set you wore the first time you had sex, when your lover kissed your eyelids and said, "Nothing will ever be as beautiful as the sight of you"? Watch your lover raise the cloth to his nose and inhale so deeply the cotton clings to the nostrils of your lover's—

. . . your lover's . . .

. . . your . . . *ex*-lover's . . .

. . .

Abandon your shopping basket and back away.

Veronique Offered a Toe

Yet the mysterious rabbit was not satisfied with such a paltry morsel. A toe? With a nail as thick as the bark of the hundred-year-old trees around him? He didn't know attached to that toe's horny nail was lovely pink flesh, smoothed by pumice, oiled by lanolin, and it was this, really, that Veronique had offered, drawn to the rabbit by its fluorescent blue fur and its lime green nose.

I got to have me a bunny like this, she thought.

How might such an animal have come to the woods behind her tiny farmhouse, she wondered, but not for long, for her mind raced even as her foot was poised in offering.

How to lure this bunny home?

Veronique was no stranger to seductions of one sort or another. At a young age, she had seduced first her brother, then her father, then the town into thinking they had been the seducers. In shame they had fled, leaving her the farmhouse and herself to care for. No more smelly-as-bears men to force her to cook and wash from dawn to dusk. Herself, she washed in the rain or the icy river at the edge of the woods. She ate only light meals of wild lettuce and grass, of herbs and berries, all rife in her woods both summer and winter. It did not occur to her that these would be better offerings to the multicolored rabbit than her own sweet foot. Surely a rabbit of this caliber would need something more, something of substance.

And she was not wrong. This rabbit had sharp incisors and thick molars. This rabbit liked meat, and he had the jaws to prove it. He did so on Veronique's toe, biting beyond the joint, at which point the entire foot, ankle, calf, and thigh became visible to the rabbit, who felt love, or lust. Desire. Thirst.

Veronique had only slightly flinched at the dismemberment of her digit. In fact, she kept her foot raised, allowing the blood to flow freely down the throat of the cottontail, transfusing him, transforming him.

It took a moment for her blood to enter his bloodstream, but once it had, Veronique watched the metamorphosis with awe. His fur shed like late-autumn leaves in a fierce wind, exposing skin the color of chestnuts. His ears shrunk, only a finger longer than her own. His haunches grew to legs, his paws to hands, the fingers stubby but multi-jointed. His face, no longer the simpering snout of a rabbit, was as human as her own, and lovelier still than any she had seen beyond her own reflection from the river's surface.

"Carry me home," she said, raising her injured foot, "since it's for you I'm an invalid."

He did, lifting her, light as a feather, looking forward to all she would offer him. How foolish he had been to think she would offer only a toe. She had spilled blood for him. She had made a man of him. He would stay with her always.

Back at the farmhouse, he lay her in bed and lay with her, their lovemaking oiled by the blood still seeping from her foot and the musk oozing from his pores. After, he slept peacefully, a tiny bunny nuzzling against his littermates. When he awoke in the morning, she was gone, a trail of blood leading out the door and into the woods. He followed it to the riverbank, where he saw her on the other side, licking her fluorescent pink fur and lime green nose.

When she saw him, she hesitated only a moment before bolting, limping only a very little bit as she bulleted through the woods, her ears back, her fur flying—she was freedom itself.

She was gone.

He looked then at his man's body, now needing a shave and a bath and animal flesh to keep it going. He ran his hands over the hairless skin of his chest.

He dropped to his knees, aching at the bend, cried out in a not quite human voice but with a sound of agony he could ever have contained in his small rabbit body.

"Not enough. Not enough."

How Good and How Simple

"He also wanted to say, 'Forgive,' but said 'Forgo,' and, no longer able to correct himself, waved his hand, knowing the one who had to would understand."
—*The Death of Ivan Ilyich*, Leo Tolstoy

"His heart was going like mad and yes I said yes I will Yes"
—Molly Bloom, *Ulysses*, James Joyce

Naked from the waist up, arms flung over his head, Walter's torso flung too, down, onto his bed, perpendicular to the direction one usually assumes on a mattress, as if while seated there on the edge of the bed, in the room in which he has spent decades of nights with two wives, *spent* in the truest sense of the word, having finished each woman in her own way, one to a desperate divorce, one to a cancerous death, as if finally, after trudging the mountain of stairs, having gotten himself seated, he simply let his muscles and ligaments and spine give up, give in, and collapse, which is exactly what he did moments ago, with the room spinning, not from drink as in his youth, but from the very gyrational nature of Earth itself, gravity taking over, taking him, flinging him to supine as he and those women had flung themselves, so many times over so many years, onto this bed, fully naked then, taking each other to places, oh, yes, yes, the places they went, yes.

Despite appearances, specifically despite the appearance at the foot of his bed of his daughter—a middle-aged woman herself now, for Christ's sake—his first child, fifty years old, married, a career woman with a sense of humor to match his own, but dry, drier—despite her having ventured up those same stairs to stand at the foot of the bed, despite her peering at him, clearly disturbed by his half-nakedness, by his *flungness*, hell, disturbed at simply being in the bedroom of her pre-divorced parents, the bedroom of her childhood parents, for in the divorce he had kept the house, he had *built* this house after all, built this room, a room she, the daughter, the child, was never allowed into uninvited and, let's face it, has avoided like dog shit on the sidewalk since she was five and got an eyeful when she rushed in unannounced one Thanksgiving morning to scream, "The turkey's on fire!" as wife number one, her mother, but his wife after all, moaned from quite a different peaking fire—despite how he must look to her, this child-woman, look as if he's lazily sleeping in the middle of a fine summer day, the kind of day he once would have spent pulling in the first cut of hay from the fields, or spent on skis skimming across the smooth surface of an up-north lake, the kind of afternoon he would have inhaled until his lungs were whales busting for air, his profound Polish proboscis sucking in the scents of shorn alfalfa, ozone, motor oil, the smoke of a steak smoking on a hot grill half-a-mile away or right there on the patio he'd poured himself—

despite the child, the woman, his daughter, nervously leaning over him now, her hands clasping and unclasping,
reminding him of a cat pawing at the spot where a bug disappeared into the earth—despite his woman-daughter
studying him *flung* into this animalistic state of collapse and
muscular abandon—despite the appearance that he's the
idle, lazy boy his ma had always claimed he was, certain he
would do nothing with his life, that he's done, is doing, will
do, nothing ever—despite what may or may not be his in-
dolent nature—Ma was right, he could have, should have
done more—despite all he appears to be, he's working . . .
huhhhh . . . working . . . *huhhh* . . . hard to breathe.

He's deeply engaged in his current life's work, breathing, his primary daily activity, which occupies the majority
of his waking and sleeping hours amid this cyclone of
thoughts, the whirlwind of ideas, impressions, images,
which both distract him from his work and keep him at it,
keep him working, working hard, keep him, keep him, him,
him, *hhuhh,* him *breathing.*

Will he continue?

The question settles like a fat trout on his chest.

Another wet fish soaking him (or is that his own cold
sweat smearing him?):

Should he?

Keep . . . huhhh . . .

No Olympic athlete training on this perfect afternoon
is working harder than Walter, the gray tendrils of his chest
hair sodden, his whitefish flesh stretched to bust, his violent triple-bypass scar a scarlet road across his chest plate,
branding him with the memory of a surgery that severed
his pectoral muscles, ending his accordion playing for

good, a devastating blow to a man who chased the next opportunity to play like a Jack Russell on the scent of a squirrel. He finger-taps the scar now as if it were the little post-bypass keyboard he brought to the jams at Bernice's Danceland on Thursday nights, not the same as fronting, not the same at all, no longer playing the melody, hiding in the harmony, having to defer to the squeeze-man, the star as he'd been for so many years, making do as *part* of the band, on stage at least, doing all right, singing lead vocals when one of the boys needed a break, his baritone voice as strong as hair-on-your-chest coffee, the kind Ma made for him on ten-below winter mornings when he longed for chest hair, wet or dry, not just a sign that manhood had finally visited him, but any goddamn thing to keep him warm until shoveling the manure from the horses' stalls heated him enough he didn't think his toes were detaching from his foot, his fingers snapping from his hands.

This breathing business is different work though.

Should he choose to stay at it, to stay, he'll need to con-centrate, to listen not just to the beat but to the back beat, arrhythmic as it is. *Should he?* Is anything left for him in this life, any surprise, something he can't imagine until it pounces on him, some joy like holding this cat-pawing daughter-child's mewling body for the first time, or a fresh tune reminding him of falling leaves, or horse breath steaming from fat silken nostrils, a downy nose nuzzling his shoulder, winter hair thick beneath his frozen fingers, or wife one, trailing her fingers down his neck, wife two, rubbing soreness from his shoulders? All good, but even devastation could spark desire, such as when he found his Rocky, his old boxer-shepherd mix, who'd been with him longer than this daughter-baby then, a dead heap next to the food dish he'd fashioned from Pa's pickup's hubcap, the poor animal almost certainly poisoned by that son-of-a-bitch Fred Garrish, revenge for the back-pasture dispute, SOB had to kill something, would have jumped for joy seeing Walter muddying that same back-pasture soil with tears, digging the grave, gathering the fur body in his arms, so familiar in Walter's hands, the ol' boy liked a good scratch down the spine, the dog's bones more familiar than his ma's, so he's not ashamed to say he cried more laying the animal into the earth than when his mother was laid to rest.

Maybe surprise crouches, like the taste of the sushi his daughter had brought him last week, daring him to try it, "Once before you die?" she'd joked, then coughed the joke out, leaving the trueness of her statement chasing the emptiness raging through the house's rooms, the house he had built for the full life of a young man and a middle-aged man, not an old man, the stairs a challenge, the quiet causing his breath to roar. Such an effort, sweating like that salted pig on a spit at the luau his pal Lawrence threw, what, forty, fifty—Christ, yes—fifty years ago when eating a piece of salted and oiled meat the size of your head meant you'd grabbed a little of the good life, and he'd said, "Yes, yes," greedy and salivating as Lawrence sliced a fat piece of loin just for him, slapped it onto a plate already heaped with buttered potatoes and coleslaw and an ear of sweet corn from Walter's own field.

Course he hasn't worked the land for years, decades really, shocking, given how much dirt he's raked from his fingernails, good work, real work, mostly, before the corporations, not that land wasn't always a business, he knew that, his Pa knew too, no big shots either of them, nothing like the branch of the family working the northern land, but he'd done all right, had kept everyone fed, got kids to eighteen when he'd let them off the chain to run, horses bolting in a lightning storm.

"You okay, Dad?" he vaguely hears the daughter say, but he's still tasting that corn, the rich pork fat, the cooling coleslaw, none of which he could eat today, not in this condition, and anyway there's no one left to make it for him, Lawrence long dead, his brother too, all the boys he played in the band with gone, Hank and Fritz, who died on stage, Nigel and his magic sax, all gone, the wives too, both before him, defying statistics, leaving him to die alone.

That's what it's come to, he supposes.

"Dad, are you okay?" A prayer from some dim place, a mile or more beyond the breath he's managed to scrape into the sac in his chest. The daughter's hands burn him, trying to press something plastic to his mouth. Is she trying to kill him, save him? He pushes her away, won't let her call the tune on his last breath—"Oxygen, Dad"—so like her mother—"Oxygen"—*his* breath alone, *his* choice to make, or not, as he sees fit. He won't be dictated to, not in his own goddamn house, won't be smothered as she'd done by tethering him to that woman who didn't really love him, whom he didn't love much himself except that he loved her more than anyone in some ways, in some ways she knew him best, young him, the boy who'd turned into a man, not easily, with the violence of that twister smashing through the back hay loft, both of them babies themselves when the girl came, strong as any of the boys to come after her, headstrong as any of her brothers, his sons, one of whom wrestles him now with more strength than the kid had managed as a teenager when he'd tried to leave the house without permission, when Walter had to jerk the truck keys from the boy's hands to keep him home, which hadn't really worked, the kid storming off on foot, wiping angry tears as Walter wiped the spit the kid had gunned at his cheek. He'd been proud of the kid for standing his ground. Never told him. Or that he'd done about the same to his father at about the same age. Meant to tell him, meant to, now, got to tell him, now or—

He wrenches open his eyelids. The man's face above him is so like the boy he once knew, a son who spit in his face, threw his whole life back at him, claimed he owed nothing to the man who gave him *hhuhh . . . hhuhh . . .* breath *. . . hhuhh . . .* the struggle's reversed. The boy, strong as a man, can jerk the keys from him, shove him onto a path the way he'd tried to shove the boy all those years ago. Christ, the kid wants to smother, overpower—"Oxygen, for fuck's sake, Dad!"—him, force him to fucking live! He won't have it, won't give . . . the satisfaction . . . won't . . . unless he goddamn — *hhuhh* — wants to.

"I'm calling the ambulance." The girl . . . always a tattler . . . so like her mother.

"Wait! Just hold on." The boy . . . a confident . . . cocky . . . a bronco . . . never told him . . . proud . . . so proud of . . .

"Did you hear? . . . Dad? . . . She's calling now . . . unless . . . Dad?"

The boy's eyes, Walter's own blue eyes but more his wife's eyes, who sometimes looked at him in just this way, begging him *not* to go to the music she hated, not one more drink, no more women, pleading stay, stay, stay, the boy—

"Tell me what to do, Dad."

Oh.

"Dad—"

Imagine.

"Tell me."

After all this time. His boy wants his father to tell him what to do. Wonders never do cease. Isn't life full of surprises. On a hot day like this, with his daughter here, such a good girl, always, when his son has finally looked at him, looked *to* him, finally . . . enough . . .

Yes.

All that's left. To say.

"Can't live—*hhuhh*—like thi—*hhuhh*—ssss."

Holding onto those blue eyes, which hold him as he once held his Rocky, nodding, and—*oh, look!*—weeping, don't cry, oh, my poor son, my boy, it will all be—*hhuhh*—just*hhuhh*—just black,

black, black, black, black, black, black, black, black, black,
black, black, black, black, black, black, black, black, black,
black, black, black, black, black, black, black, black, black,
black, black, black, black, black, black, black, black, black,
black, black, black, black, black, black, black, black, black,
black, black, black, black, black, black, black black, black,
black, black, black, black, black, black, black, black, black,
black, black, black, black, black,

Acknowledgments

I have written the stories in this collection over a span of three decades. The influences on my sense of what makes a story have been so vast and varied I can't possibly account for them all. That said, I do want to acknowledge a few folks specifically. First, I want to thank every student who has taken a creative writing class with me. Together we have worked out what stories are, how they work, and how they are ever-changing beasts. It has been my honor and pleasure to talk writing with you: Hello, Writers!

I would like to acknowledge Rhode Island College, the Rhode Island College Foundation, and the Rhode Island College Alumni Affairs Office for their support.

I thank the editors and publishers of the journals who have given my stories opportunities to be read. Your hidden work deserves to be acknowledged more.

Most especially, I want to thank Bill Burleson and Flexible Press for the integrity, joy, and enthusiasm brought to my writing. You have been a true home for so many writers, and for me in particular. Your efforts and energy are unique and extraordinary in the world of publishing, and I count myself lucky to be an FP writer.

I extend my sincere thanks to the friends and family who read, and tell others to read, my writing. It means so very much.

Special thanks to my siblings, who always go the extra mile in their enthusiasm and efforts to get my work out there. A little sister can have no greater joy than making her big siblings proud.

Finally, to Paul, who is my true home. I'm so lucky to have found my way to you.

About the Author

Karen Lee Boren is the author of the books *Secret Waltz* (2022 Flexible Press), an Independent Press Award Distinguished Favorite; *Mother Tongue* (2016 New Rivers Press); and *Girls in Peril* (2006 Tin House Press), a Barnes and Noble Discover selection. She has been nominated for a Pushcart Prize. Among other places, her fiction and nonfiction appears in *Notre-Dame Review*, *WomenArts Journal*, *Santa Fe Writer's Project*, *The Florida Review*, *New South*, *Hawai'i Pacific Review*, *BookForum*, *Litro*, and *The Best of Lonely Planet's Travel Writing*. She's earned an M.F.A. from Wichita State University and a Ph.D. from the University of Wisconsin-Milwaukee. She is a professor at Rhode Island College. She lives and writes in Providence.

9 7 9 8 9 9 1 4 9 2 8 6 7